THE BOOK SYNDICATE IN ISTANBUL

OMER GOK

Copyright © 2025 OMER GOK

All rights reserved.

To old friends —

scattered across forgotten cities,

lost in time,

carried away by life's invisible winds.

We do not see each other.

We do not hear each other.

Yet somewhere,

somehow,

we still walk the same streets in dreams.

This book is for you.

1

One of the worst students in the history of "Middle East Technical University's Faculty of Architecture, Department of Architecture" was trying to graduate. It was difficult. He was in his sixth year at the school, and the accumulation of years was almost preventing him from breaking the American game called the cumulative system. The cumulative system was a cruel system that wanted people to carry the mistakes they made in the past for almost a lifetime, cursing their fate. Its aim wasn't to rehabilitate the guilty, but to write their crime on a board and hang it around their neck as a warning to others. To put it simply so everyone can understand: passing classes wasn't enough to graduate; you also needed to get very high grades to repair past mistakes and bring your overall average above 2. So what was this 2? 2 was half of the full grade, the full grade being 4, but 2 wasn't half of 100. According to one rumor, 2 was equivalent to 70 out of 100, but this 70 was also variable and relative; even 70 wasn't really 70 anymore, if you understand. I couldn't figure out how this was possible in six years, and I don't expect you to understand it here, but I should say that the system not only continuously punished you but also devalued your mind with its irrationality. Having a grade point average of 2 wasn't enough; it had to be a value above 2. For example, theoretically, there are infinite numbers greater than 2 between 2 and 2.1. However, the smallest value permitted by the system's irrationality was 2.02. And I was one of the rare lucky ones who managed to graduate with this average.

2

So why was this graduation so difficult? I may not tell or be able to tell the answer to this question in this book! This book has changed many times, is changing, starting again and again. This will continue until it ends. When it's finished, its beginning and end will be clear. I might have given clues to all this in the first book.

Second question: now that I've graduated, was it a good thing? Can one approach history with such a question? We have many choices in our lives; our paths don't split into just two or three, but sometimes branch out like a tree into dozens of paths, and we can't know how we entered which path. Fate, God, will, the will of others, mere coincidences, determination by chaos, determination by science, the Devil's work—we don't know, we can't know, and we ask. That's why I'm asking whether it was good or bad. Events that seem terrible at the time, that feel like the end of the world, can be perceived differently as time passes. Presumably everyone knows the story of Khidr and Moses in the Quran. In our lives, Khidr always goes ahead and shapes our destiny. If you ask God, all these things direct us toward the good, the true, the beautiful, and the beneficial. If you ask people, they say "Why so much pain?" The perception of one who suffers the pain is different. Is it God's lack of these emotions that makes things difficult for us? He doesn't understand us... Good and bad thus lose their meaning and definition.

3

I didn't experience the same bad luck in finding a job that I had during my school life and graduation. In fact, I received a job offer while I was still begging for grades to graduate. My friend Tolga, whom I had worked with during an internship, called me. He had joined a construction company, and they were looking for a newly graduated architect. I had submitted my project and had time to spare, so I could work. I went for the interview. The deputy general manager was a graduate of METU Architecture and was a good man, but I didn't like the boss—he was quite arrogant. But I thought, "He's the boss, it can happen," and let it go. We quickly came to an agreement, and I started work. Since the company was constantly getting new projects and was in a growth phase, they were looking for new staff. I recommended a friend from school, Türker, and he also came and started. We all worked in one room. We only had one final submission left, for the detailing course. I never liked it—actually, I never liked any course. Working at this company had been helpful; we invited another friend, stayed up all night, and prepared the submission drawings. We had the company's resources at our disposal and completed the work very quickly. The submission was made, and I no longer had any responsibilities related to school. Now our only job was real life.

4

The task assigned to me was to make preliminary preparations for a newly acquired project. The job was the renovation and repair of the American Consulate in Istanbul. The work hadn't started yet, and I spent my early days reading through tender documents—I wasn't idle, there were hundreds and thousands of pages in front of me, and I read them all. All the documents and projects were in English. I kept a dictionary by my side, but it wasn't enough, so I also bought a technical terms dictionary. I was figuring it out. Others were doing different jobs—support team for projects in Russia, drawings, procurement... the endless work of construction companies. The Deputy General Manager, Ahmet, was directly involved with my project. Ahmet was truly a nice man, too nice...

It had been about a month since I started working, and I had practically memorized all the documents; the work was about to begin. A foreman from Çorum was finding the teams. The foreman had started coming to the office, sitting with Ahmet to discuss team numbers and what types of craftsmen would be needed. I also participated in these conversations, continuously learning. It was almost like on-the-job training.

The time to start work had come, but the site manager designated for this job couldn't return from Russia. The work there was both extending and the contract was growing. It wasn't clear when he would return. They were saying he might be back in a few months.

5

Ahmet would temporarily take over the job, it seemed, as the site handover date was approaching. It was in a few days. Ahmet was making his preparations, and I was supporting him as much as I could. We were having a small meeting about the job, discussing the work schedule, labor schedule, and so on. "It would be good for you to come too—you'll see the site, it'll be better," he said. I was happy; I hadn't been to Istanbul for a while, and I hadn't really gone back and forth much anyway—I had worked at exhibitions for two summers, that was all...

Ahmet had a house in a strange location in Istanbul, or at least it seemed strange to me at the time. The location was very close to work. The American Consulate was in Tepebaşı, and the house was in Çukurcuma. If you walk from Taksim toward Tünel, after a while you'll see Ağa Mosque on your right; enter the street directly across from it—back then this street was full of bars and nightclubs—then continue down this street, which initially slopes down gently, but toward the end, the slope becomes steeper, an adverse ramp. Let yourself go down this adverse ramp, let your legs chase each other, involuntarily descend downward—I forgot to mention, but at the beginning of this ramp, look straight ahead, because Ahmet's house is on the third floor of the building directly across, it almost comes to eye level from there. This street is called Sadri Alışık Street, and Ahmet's house is at the intersection of Sadri Alışık Street and Turnacıbaşı Avenue, the building across, don't forget. I'll return to this neighborhood and area again, I'll have to return, because I would be living there in the coming days...

6

Yes, work was starting, but getting into the American Consulate wasn't so easy; there was a detailed security check, and since my coming hadn't been planned, the necessary documents for this security check hadn't been submitted. Therefore, my entry took quite a long time. The consulate was a beautiful, historic building, in one of the best locations in Tepebaşı. The Pera Palace Hotel was on one side, and the other side overlooked the Golden Horn. Inside was a kind of American territory. A line suddenly made us guests in our own country. Then doors, searches... First a small security window, then a guardhouse attached to the outer wall. Passing through there was difficult. Searches, screenings... Then another room in the building, more searching and screening there, from place to place... And finally, all borders are crossed, and you enter.

7

The first contractor had been an American company. Everyone knows Morrison, our Morrison. Morrison Süleyman's company. This company had subcontracted the job to a Turkish company. And we were İmeks's subcontractor, meaning we were the subcontractor's subcontractor. Like the last hole in a zurna, but we would be doing all the work, bearing the entire burden. When we entered, we first went to our primary contractor İmeks's office, which was a container. We sat down, explained our plan, and chatted a bit. Ahmet was subdued, and I was silent. Our plan was clearly lousy... We didn't have a single worker; they would be coming from Çorum. Foreman

Tuncay would bring the men. There was no mobilization or preparation visible. The men needed a place to stay, they needed food, they needed tools. Ahmet and I had brought the projects and contract under our arms to Istanbul. We spent that day there, leaving toward evening...

Ahmet was a person who enjoyed eating and drinking, especially drinking and tavern conversations. Upon leaving, he said, "Let's go to Cumhuriyet." Tepebaşı and its surroundings were rich in taverns. We walked to Cumhuriyet, with our bags in our hands. Ahmet was a good architect and site manager, but more importantly, he was a good intellectual, which is why we got along quickly. He liked me, and I genuinely liked him too; I respected him. He ordered simple and essential appetizers. "Small fish goes with rakı," he would say. This was our first tavern conversation, and it was repeated dozens of times afterward. We didn't drink much, but our moods were good, and when we left, we went to the house in Çukurcuma.

8

This house was truly a very old house and had never been renovated. Another surprise awaited me in the house. A friend of Ahmet's was staying there—his name was Tamer, a tour guide. He was a strange one. We chatted a bit. We arranged a place for me to sleep. There wasn't a part of the house that wasn't falling apart. Fortunately, I would only be staying for a few days, so we would manage.

The first three days passed doing the same things: we would get up in the morning, get dressed, and leave immediately. Since we were somewhat hungover, we would either be already late or about to be late. Actually, there wasn't any urgent work to do, but we wanted to arrive on time to show that we were disciplined. Then, we would either go directly to İstiklal Street from Sadri Alışık or reach Galatasaray from Turnacıbaşı, grab a pastry from somewhere before reaching Odakule, pass through Odakule to Tepebaşı, and from there to the consulate. The contractor firm had allocated a room in the prefabricated building for us. All day we would work there on plans and schedules. Occasionally there would be meetings with the contractor. At noon we would go out for lunch; Ahmet could sit in a tavern even at lunchtime and eat fish, with one or two double rakıs on the side. I was hesitant to drink, sometimes taking just one shot to accompany him. Then we would return around 3-4, hang around for a few more hours, and leave. Again we would sit somewhere, sometimes Ahmet's friends from Istanbul would join us, and then we would return to the crumbling house. On the fourth day, when we arrived at the office, Ahmet's face had turned serious; he moved his chair closer to me, then took a breath and adjusted his jacket upward, "I'll be returning to Ankara today; I have some work there for about a week. I'd like you to manage things here for a week. Foreman Tuncay is coming today; you can plan some things with him. I'll be here until the evening, and when he arrives, the three of us can sit and discuss what to do. Also, submit your documents for the security check in the meantime. Just in case. Okay?" he said with a smile on his face. There was a feeling of embarrassment on his face for having to do something like this, even if unintentionally. "Okay, fine, but I didn't bring enough clothes," I said. "I'll leave you some money, you can buy some things for yourself," he replied. "Okay," I said without prolonging it. I was both excited and scared; I would be doing a job I had never done before, even if only for a while. In an unfamiliar city, and in its most lively, most dangerous, most entertaining part. Things were easy when Ahmet was around. I would follow Ahmet wherever he went. Now I would have to plan my life myself.

9

Foreman Tuncay had arrived in the afternoon. His security clearance had been processed, and paperwork for all the workers he would bring had been submitted two months ago. He entered much more easily than I did. Tuncay was a short, bald-headed man—though he usually wore a cap—dark and wiry. You couldn't tell if he was telling the truth or lying, if he was good or bad; he was an inscrutable type, but he knew his job. In a few days, workers would start arriving, they needed accommodation, their food issues needed to be resolved, they needed clothing. Ahmet was giving suggestions: "Do this, do that," as he was leaving anyway; these tasks would fall on us. The foreman and I looked at each other, then the foreman would say to Ahmet, "Boss, we'll handle everything." I couldn't say it; I had never handled these things before. When the foreman said these things to Ahmet, Ahmet would turn to me and give some warnings in his own way. Ahmet left before evening. The foreman and I sat in the office a bit longer. He was calling me "boss," which surprised me. I was 24, the foreman was about 40. It was strange for him to call me "boss." Around five o'clock, I went to the contractor's site manager's room. The site manager was an electrical engineer, a man with a bushy mustache and a workaholic type. I sat with him for a while, then said, "We're leaving now; workers will be arriving the day after tomorrow, and we'll be picking up the pace." "Okay, okay, you can go," he said. The foreman and I left the consulate. "Boss, I'm going to my hotel; I've found an inexpensive place around here," he said. "Okay, see you tomorrow," I said. I left the foreman and walked toward İstiklal...

10

Without Ahmet, it was difficult. I used to follow behind him; now I was alone and had to do whatever I wanted by myself. My feet weren't heading home; the house was gloomy—an antique house with high ceilings, but the furniture, doors, woodwork, and wooden floor were older than old. And there was Tamer in the house; where had this Tamer come from? If he weren't there, if I were alone, I would feel more comfortable. At least I was also temporary. Ahmet had said, "I'll come back in a week at the latest, then we'll see." I hadn't taken the route through Odakule; lost in thought as I was walking, I had missed it and continued straight ahead, passing in front of the Büyük Lodra Hotel and going toward the fish market through a side street. This road was neither gloomy nor dark. The buildings were derelict, their doors nailed shut with planks. I passed through the street selling tourist souvenirs and collectibles at the fish market, walking a bit more slowly and looking around. I was holding my bag, which was making me uncomfortable. Thinking of dropping the bag off at the house, I quickened my pace. I passed Nevizade so quickly that the head waiters couldn't even invite me to the empty tables on the street. It was truly difficult without Ahmet; I was alone, afraid of my loneliness. When I reached İstiklal, I slowed down, hoping to perhaps see some familiar faces. Maybe someone from Ankara, who knows? I continued walking, the crowd was flowing. I was looking at women—their walks, their jeans, their skirts, their hair, their attitudes, their styles... I was desiring them, but I was distant, in an invisible glass jar. I felt like a hardened criminal. I was passing by stands selling Beyoğlu chocolate, with one eye on the vendor. Years later, I would buy so many chocolates from here. I was passing İnci, profiterole. We would sit here so much together and eat quickly. We would have them pack a kilo to take home, but I didn't know all this yet as I was walking. I was just a young, crazy man, unable to see the future...

11

When I reached Sadri Alışık Street, I stopped. I said I would return here. Turning onto this street from İstiklal meant returning to that time. Returning to our story. Entering a time tunnel.

It was 1997, and it was July when Ahmet left me in Istanbul.

Although Ahmet had said "I'll be back in a week," he didn't return; he came two weeks later. During this period, we continued our phone conversations. Usually he would call me, and occasionally I would call him. I had become permanent in my temporary job. Site manager Haluk Efendi was supposed to come from Russia; we were still waiting. The uncertainty would continue until he arrived.

The first stop on Sadri Alışık Street was **Lades** Restaurant. If you ever find yourself here, don't be surprised that there are two Lades facing each other. They're not the same, but different, like the wishbone. I was surprised. When you enter the street, the restaurant on the right is where you eat lunch, with its spotlessly clean white tablecloths and the best place for traditional dishes. In the window display, you'll see huge jars of jams and pickles. These are the colors of the restaurant. Of course, Ahmet had introduced me to this place too. Ahmet was my guide and had become my friend over time. At Lades, we would either sit and order, or go inside to the kitchen and choose our meals. It was here that I first ate artichoke with its stem. Lades would be crowded at lunchtime; nice people would come, the chefs were polite, Lades was like Ahmet, or perhaps I had merged Lades with Ahmet. The restaurant across the street was a breakfast place, with Istanbul's most delicious pan-fried eggs and various types of menemen omelets. Those who wanted could also get honey and cream, cheese and olives as supplements, and a fresh white loaf cut into quarters would be placed on the table in those days. There was no limit to bread, and the double tea came in water glasses. I would sometimes meet Foreman Tuncay here in the mornings; he loved this place because you could eat plenty and get full, and in the end, you'd pay very little.

(For the working class, the most important thing is being able to get full; eating is an energy accounting.)

Speaking of Foreman Tuncay, I must tell you about him.

12

If you leave this breakfast restaurant, turn right toward İstiklal, and then cross to the street directly opposite, passing by the side of Ağa Mosque, your path will be cut by the boulevard. Cross the boulevard too, and the neighborhood on the other side is Tarlabaşı. Tarlabaşı was important to us because that's where we solved the accommodation problem for the workers. In those days, Tarlabaşı was truly Tarlabaşı—dangerous to some, the center of filth and crime. We fearlessly went and rented a building, then Foreman Tuncay and I bought bunk beds, mattresses, etc. from Topkapı, turning this building into a dormitory. Since everyone was in construction, the renovation work wasn't a problem. Tuncay had made a room for himself there, while the other workers stayed in rooms of 4-6 people. As the site manager, I would occasionally visit the dormitory in the evenings; the workers needed morale, and I had quickly realized that workers had childlike spirits. (But don't let this state of mind deceive you; workers are also necessarily selfish and self-interested from a class perspective. They can stab you in the back when you least expect it.) The streets in Tarlabaşı were always crowded, colorful—Gypsies, Kurds, transvestites, washed-up prostitutes, street-smart hustlers, drug dealers, users, hustlers, vendors—everyone was there. I used to be afraid at first, but later I got used to it. Stuffed mussels were made in basements, and they smelled bad. Now a group of construction workers had also entered this life, and this was a complex situation; I had to go in and learn. While having breakfast with the foreman at Lades, it was easy to get information from him. I would learn secrets about the workers during such times, when the foreman was either digging into a large piece from the loaf, tackling the honey and cream, or when his mouth was full of menemen: "Boss," he would start while trying to swallow his bite quickly... (Experience was also needed to separate the lies from the truth, and in those days, I didn't have that...)

13

The second stop on this street was the börek shop, right next to Lades. The börek shop generally shared my morning solitude. It was a tiny shop with its counter right in front of the outward-facing window, positioned to both tempt those outside and provide quick service to those who entered. When you went in, the counter was on the left, and along the right wall ran a narrow bench-like counter. The remaining space held four small tables with two chairs at each. It was here that I first ate "empty börek"—a pastry with nothing inside, sprinkled with powdered sugar, which I would eat with hot milk on cold mornings to warm myself. Poğaças were served sliced at the börek shop, with a piece of yellow straw paper placed on the metal plate. This absorbed the oil from the greasy böreks and poğaças, so the plates wouldn't get too dirty. Sometimes I would be indecisive at the börek shop, unable to decide what to eat. In such cases, I would eat mixed börek, half with minced meat and half with cheese, and instead of milk, I would drink a double tea. Water börek was heavy, and I rarely ate it. The börek shop warmed me up, which is why I always came here alone.

Pausing the street tour, I want to return to the **consulate**. After Ahmet left, workers started arriving—first 7 people, then 9, then more, and at the peak, we reached up to 30 people. Because of the security check, I had trouble entering for the first month. The completion of the investigation was increasingly delayed. Despite having no crimes or criminal record, my general state of guilt and my feelings made me uneasy. I thought about impossible things, most troubling were the leftist demonstrations I had participated in at university. Although I had never been detained during these demonstrations, I thought, "What if they have a record on me?" These Americans investigate deeply; what if they found this record? I was suspicious of myself, but in the end, the investigation was completed, and I came out clean. I was greatly relieved; now I had my ID badge and could easily enter the consulate as a regular employee. The job was an easy one, but difficult for me. It was my first job, and I was very inexperienced and novice. I would learn something in the evening and sell it the next morning to keep the job going, but sometimes this system would falter. My greatest advantage was that I had studied the project very well. I probably knew the project better than anyone. English was becoming a problem. I had realized two things: The technical knowledge taught at school was almost nothing, and the English used at school had no relation to real life. The project involved a certain complexity; we were closing the building section by section, making temporary spaces before closures—it was more of an operation than construction. I had good relations with the Americans and generally didn't have problems.

14

And back to the street... When you exit the börek shop and head downward, Sadri Alışık Street begins to liven up. On the left was the street's first nightclub, which we oddly avoided and never entered. We saw it as a trap, though I always had a curiosity about the place, but we were hesitant to try it...

Continuing on, on the right side was one of the most important rock bars of that time. I would hang out there on evenings when I was alone; beer and tequila were cheap there. This bar was black inside and out—everywhere was black—with girls dressed in black with long hair hanging out there. I would sit in a corner for hours with a beer in my hand. As the night progressed and people got tipsy, there would be swaying. Long-haired, purple-eyed rocker girls would only hook up with boys who looked like them, but I would push the boundaries if I had drunk enough. I had become acquainted with the bartender over time; they would always let me in because I drank well and a lot, and after an hour I would buy drinks for the girls too.

Let's leave this boring black bar and continue. A little further ahead, in a dead-end side street, you'll see the Beyoğlu Police Station. This location always seemed strange and absurd to me for a police station. The police were almost invisible, just guests in this chaotic, cosmopolitan street. After passing the police station, the entertainment level rises, and nightclubs and cheap hotels where prostitutes stay begin...

15

Every time I passed through this street, after passing the police station, I would see a tavern-like place entered through a kind of passage and visible from outside, resembling the taverns in old Turkish films, and I always wondered about it. But to be able to describe this place to you, I first need to tell you about Ela. Ela is one of the most important figures in the Istanbul chapter. In fact, the most important:

Ela

n. (ela:) 1. Chestnut color that tends toward yellow in the eye. 2. *adj.* That which has this color:* "Fair one with hazel eyes whom I love / Since I've not seen you, I've longed to see you"* -Karacaoğlan.

(*Contemporary Turkish Dictionary*)

Ela is a three-letter word, its meaning is above.

After several months had passed, the work at the consulate had increased; besides field work, we needed to prepare and submit a lot of shop drawings. And the job didn't end there—purchasing, workers' problems, meetings—a construction site was an endless workload. The most dramatic aspect was that I was alone in charge. Ahmet was also aware that I needed an assistant. A few weeks later he called me, saying he would come to Istanbul. I was happy; the loneliness had really started to bother me.

16

Ahmet called the day he arrived, saying he was in the lobby of the Pera Palace. I rushed outside. When I arrived—sometimes we would meet here before he went inside, discuss work matters, and he would get a report from me before entering—we were going to do the same, I thought. Ahmet was sitting at a table in the back. I could see him from the side; there was someone across from him, I couldn't see clearly, but I sensed it was a woman. I went to them and greeted them. Ahmet said "ah!" with a smile and stood up. The woman sitting across from him also stood up. She was a very thin, dark girl, almost skeletal. She had straight hair cut bluntly just below her ears. After Ahmet's lengthy introduction ceremony, everyone sat back down. He began to talk at length about Ela. Ela was an architect, the daughter of close family friends, and he had known her almost since childhood. He explained that he was thinking of having Ela work as my assistant. Actually, they had already agreed on this and finalized it. To not offend me, as if it would happen with my approval too, he said, "I'm thinking." I said, "Sure, sure, why not?" nodding my head. Ela was someone who spoke softly, a bit nervous, a bit shaky, but sweetly and gently. She was also nodding in agreement with what Ahmet was saying; we all agreed on everything, but we were prolonging the conversation, unable to put a period on it. I would interject, talking about the difficulties of the job, my inability to draw formwork plans, my slowness on the computer, my inability to get away from the site. Ahmet would immediately say, "Ela will handle it." "Of course, of course," we all said together. Finally, we had clarified the issue; we all lit cigarettes, and I ordered a beer... Ela would start work next week. After Ela left, Ahmet asked, "Well?" Calmly lowering my head, I approved the situation and ordered another beer...

17

Ela adapted to the job quickly, sitting in the downstairs room assigned to us. I usually sat in the contractor's site manager's room. I would occasionally go to her, check what she was doing, and we would talk. She was a very quiet person. We generally talked about work.

After our long working hours, toward the end of one weekend, Ahmet had come. We all went out to eat; we had gone to Refik. The conversation was going well. Ela was an intellectual girl, well-read and literate... I liked this about her. The next day Ahmet came to the office around noon. We usually worked until noon on Saturdays, but that day we left around 4 in the afternoon, walking from Tepebaşı toward İstiklal. Ahmet was of the opinion that we should sit somewhere and have a couple of drinks, and I always looked favorably on this idea. Ela was undecided. Ahmet was constantly talking on the phone, occasionally stopping during his conversations while we continued walking, then we would wait for him. His leather briefcase was always in his hand, stuffed to bursting, with his phone in the other hand... When the conversation became serious, he would stop, and when he stopped, the balance of the İstiklal crowd would be momentarily disrupted. Ahmet didn't care about the crowd, and I liked this nonchalant attitude of his. Finally, the phone calls had ended, but Ahmet was thoughtful.

18

The three of us started walking side by side. The Saturday crowd on İstiklal didn't allow the three of us to walk together. Then Ahmet's phone rang again. The atmosphere had become quite tense. Ahmet angrily took out his phone. He introduced himself, paused for a moment, and suddenly his thoughtful tone softened. It was probably someone familiar; Ahmet's surprised face was smiling. I was listening to the conversation with one ear while my other ear was on Ela. Ahmet hung up the phone. Laughing, he said, "Kids, I have to leave." We asked what had happened. He said an old friend had called and he needed to see them. We had reached Galatasaray. Taxis were passing through the street that cut across İstiklal. "I'll catch one from here and go," said Ahmet. As he was getting into the taxi, he said to us, "You two hang out, enjoy yourselves." After Ahmet left, we remained silent for a while. We were both clearly embarrassed. We walked in silence, but somehow our feet had turned toward the fish market. As we were heading up to Nevizade, I asked, "What shall we do?" "I don't know," she said. "Shall we sit at Cumhuriyet?" I asked with an involuntary tone. If Ahmet hadn't left, we would have sat at Cumhuriyet anyway; Ahmet had developed a Cumhuriyet fixation. We were going there day and night. After thinking a bit, Ela approved my idea. This had made me happy. At Cumhuriyet, we found a place upstairs by the window; it was still early, and the tavern was empty. We could see the street from where we sat; it was a good spot. We ordered a small rakı, and I remembered that Ela was a good drinker. We ordered some appetizers; our tastes were similar. I prepared the first doubles; the rakı was ice cold. "Here's to your health," we said, raising our glasses. I drank almost half of my first double; Ela was also drinking well, but not as much as me. With her quivering lips... First she drew out the words, then the hazel of her eyes and the way they misted over... She was in perfect harmony with everything about her. I was discovering all the subtlety in her. Then I loved how she smoked, the way she waved her arm when explaining something—especially when she had a cigarette in her hand, I loved her arm movements even more. I loved how she took just a tiny bit of appetizer with the tip of her fork, brought it to her mouth, crushed the appetizer between her palate and tongue without opening her mouth, and how she sipped her rakı, sometimes looking into the distance, sometimes at the crowded street of the fish market, her black pants, the short leather jacket she wore over them... I loved her more as I drank. We were laughing, jumping from topic to topic, understanding each other. After each glass, we were thinking the same things. We were the same. We hadn't been able to see each other, to notice each other for days, but now we had found each other; we were the missing halves... When we left the tavern: "Where to?" said Ela. "There," I said, and she laughed. "Where?" she said. "There," I said. We wandered from bar to bar. That night she didn't come home with me though...

We kissed long and passionately, full of desire, in front of the Cultural Center. Then she left. When she was gone, I had fallen into a drunken emptiness, yet also into exhilaration. The next day I said, "Come," as there was no work. She came, we walked around Beyoğlu a bit, and I said, "Let's go home." "I shouldn't come," she said. I didn't listen; I wouldn't have; I walked toward home... We were coming down Sadri Alışık quickly...

That day, Ela and I had become lovers.

19

And back to Sadri Alışık Street... The tavern that looked like it came straight out of old Turkish films was called "Sevil's Place." Inside the passage, this small sign remained in shadow. For that reason, this sign written in a handwriting-like font was constantly illuminated with blue neon lights. We had noticed this place on our very first day, as we excitedly descended our street. In the early hours, it seemed like a tavern where people drank to the accompaniment of heavy Turkish Classical Music. As the night progressed, the music would become more festive. After a certain hour, even a plump, aging belly dancer would perform. Inside, there were always these same aging plump women. Ela and I had made pilgrimages to almost all the taverns in Beyoğlu and the surrounding area. We both loved drinking; perhaps this love of drinking brought us closer and then later separated us. One day, while debating where to go, I said, "I'm going to take you to a very special place." She was intrigued. "And it's on our way, very close to us," I said. She continued to ask curiously: "Where, where?"

"You actually know the place," I said. With a tense voice, she asked, "Where, tell me?" "Let's go to Sevil's Place, on our street," I said. "Okay, let's go," Ela replied.

20

It was a warm day. Ela was wearing a sleeveless top with something light over it. I was dressed as usual: jeans and a short-sleeved shirt. When we entered, all faces turned to us. It was evening. There was only one empty table. It was immediately noticeable when we entered—a table at the edge of the wall... For some reason, everyone was very surprised by our entrance, and we were surprised by their surprise. The waiter came a bit late. "How's that, a different place, isn't it?" I asked. "I don't know, this place seems a bit strange to me," she said dismissively. "I found the only venue in all of Beyoğlu that's left from old Turkish films, and I brought you here," I boasted. Ela lit a cigarette; she always smoked before meals. I wouldn't smoke during meals, and even with drinks I smoked very little. Finally, the head waiter had arrived and was looking at me. In a confused state, I said, "What appetizers do you have?" The head waiter listed them; the appetizer menu was weak—strained yogurt, eggplant spread, cheese, and cold cuts. We also ordered a small rakı. The rakı came with the appetizers, and I served it. We clinked our glasses and started drinking, as always, like any ordinary day. I had just picked up the rakı bottle for our second doubles when a plump, dark-skinned woman began approaching us. The place was so small that she was beside us in three steps. She came and sat at our table uninvited. We were dumbfounded, experiencing a brief stillness. With a manner that was part uncle, part street-smart, she said, "I'm Sevil." I introduced myself but didn't introduce Ela. She began staring at me intently; I was uncomfortable, and to break her gaze I said politely, "Are you the Sevil who owns this place?" "Yes, exactly, that's me," she said, then paused, took a deep breath, and turned to Ela. Squinting her eyes and trying to identify her, she asked, "Does the lady have a license?" At first I didn't understand; my perception in the dimness of the place had incredibly weakened. A few seconds later, with cold sweat running down my forehead and face, wiping it with the handkerchief I was squeezing in my hand, I said, "What license? We just came here to have a couple of drinks." Sevil, increasing her irritation, said, "Couldn't you find any other place to drink? You don't understand what kind of place this is." True, we didn't understand—we hadn't understood at all. "Then let's get the bill," I said, immediately asking for it. "That's for the best," said Sevil, rising slowly. The bill was a bit steep, but not unpayable. I put down the money, not even waiting for change, and we quickly left. Outside, I couldn't look Ela in the face out of embarrassment. We were both mortified by our naivety. But on the other hand, this tragicomic incident was making me laugh inside. I couldn't hold it in and burst out laughing. Ela was looking at me angrily out of the corner of her eye, but she couldn't suppress the awkward smile on her face. With quick steps, we again let ourselves down Sadri Alışık, toward home. In such situations, we would rush to perform the act that would make us forget everything—to make love as soon as possible.

21

After this point, Sadri Alışık Street began both to curve to the right and to steepen dramatically. I say dramatically because I had suffered greatly from the steepness of this ramp; in winter on snowy days, it was very difficult to climb, and descending was even harder.

On one of the days when I had drunk too much—I remember drinking at our rock bar—I fell at the beginning of this ramp and found myself almost at the front door of our building. I had slid that entire distance on the ice, but my whole body was shaken from hitting things left and right and somersaulting. The next day I woke up with unbearable pain. Along the edge of this steep slope, there were three more establishments I frequented. My memory has slowed down so much; there should have been four. The first three were on the right side, and the last one was on the left at the very end of the street, the corner building, which was a hotel in those days. A cheap hotel where prostitutes who worked in the nightclubs of the area stayed. From our balcony, all the balconies of this building were visible. During empty, troublesome, and long days, I would occasionally spy on this hotel. The prostitutes' colorful, tiny underwear would hang on the balconies. They would shout and yell at each other, but they had closed themselves off from the outside world except for business. This was their own internal ethic. On the right side, two of the three lined-up establishments were nightclubs, both owned by the same person—the upper one was called Bonbon and the lower one was called Babybon. Between these two nightclubs was a bar. You entered this bar through a small iron door, and its windows were painted in black and dark green colors. During the day, it was almost as dark as night inside. This place had no particular character; it wasn't a rock bar, it wasn't a dark bar, neither just young people nor middle-aged people hung out there. Whatever music someone brought would play; there was no DJ. It had only one bartender and someone who watched the door and the general order. It wasn't even clear who the owner was. There was an indifference toward the place and its customers. However, the place had one good feature: the drinks were cheap, the draught beer was more watered down than necessary, but I liked it watery. Tequila was almost the same price as beer. Sometimes there were no women inside at all; everyone who came was unsuccessful, lost, depressive. Anyone could end up here. Some days you would enter and the sexiest girls in Beyoğlu would be there; sometimes even rocker types would come. Sometimes even high school students skipping school. I would come here when I felt my worst, at my lowest, and drink either at the bar or in a corner. After midnight, the music would liven up, people would dance according to the mood of the place, the interior would gradually darken, and after that hour, this place was open to everything.

22

After these late hours, I would forget who I was; no kind of disgrace would scare me. With a beer in my hand, I would approach a woman and say, "What's up?" Some would just look at my face and move away from me, then I would approach someone else. These rejections and humiliations pleased me; I would laugh. Then I would join those dancing, stand provocatively in front of them, and dance as if in a tom-tom dance, as if in a primitive shamanic ritual. People would sometimes run away from me as if I were a madman, a lunatic, or thinking I was a clown, they would take me into their midst and dance with laughter. On such nights, I would completely forget who I was—where I worked, where I came from, my mother, my father, the school I attended—I would forget everything. I would kill the me everyone knew. While doing all these things, I wouldn't even think about the deep feeling of regret that would come after sobering up.

23

However, in the morning when I woke up with the unbearable headache, I would feel this regret, but it wouldn't help. Then I would make promises to myself not to do it again, but these promises wouldn't last very long. All this could repeat on any random day...

As for the nightclubs... Having two nightclubs so close to each other seemed strange at first glance, but there was a meaning to it. The upper one, Bonbon, was a place where higher quality prostitutes and hostesses worked, with better interior decoration. If you were going to Bonbon, you should have a substantial amount of money on you or a solid credit card. Taking a woman out from there wasn't so easy either; it required some effort and investment. There was no such thing as drinking a beer, negotiating, and leaving; you had to lavish the table, perhaps come again and again, and then maybe you could take the lady outside the nightclub. But was Babybon like that? No, it wasn't. You could enter Babybon when you were in a bad mood, have a beer at the bar—this beer was a bit more expensive than a normal bar—and buying a drink for a woman you liked was twice the price of a beer.

24

I had gone to Babybon for the first time with Ahmet and a few friends. We had set up a nice table. As time progressed a bit and our heads became pleasant, we had called girls to the table, and then toward dawn, we had all gotten up to dance halay together; we had gotten that drunk. That day we hadn't taken anyone home; I hadn't taken anyone. Then one day, I went there alone on a weekday and understood the matter. Babybon was truly the kind of place that could become addictive. Things were easy here: while drinking your beer at the bar, you would look around, choose the girl you liked, and make an arrangement with İsmail Ağa. İsmail Ağa was the manager of this nightclub, the boss, you might say. Since my house was almost directly across, it was easy. First I would go home, then I would wait, then the girl would come. Sometimes the girl would be very late, making me anxious; clearly İsmail Ağa was using the girl for hostessing in the meantime, using her as efficiently as possible was the basic principle. To illustrate the level of my disgraceful behavior, I can't pass without telling one incident. One day I was truly very drunk; I had spent all my money and was feeling desperately lonely, heading toward home. I necessarily had to pass in front of Babybon to get home; I had just enough money left in my pocket for a beer. I went in casually. Maybe it wasn't so casual; there was a feeling of loneliness eating away at me. In this state, if I entered my home, this decayed, dilapidated building, I felt I would die, disappear forever, and wander over the earth as an unsatisfied spirit. This was the feeling that made me fearless on these nights, that allowed me to enter every hole with a crazy courage. I would shamelessly open every door and look inside; I wanted to open every heart like this too, to look inside; I was looking for a mystery, a secret that I thought the whole world was hiding from me. I was in pain. That's why I entered Babybon. Whether it was from this crazy courage or from the protection of drunkenness, or perhaps because God had taken pity on me and assigned one of his angels to protect me, who knows... In nights that lasted until dawn, I hadn't received even a single flick; I would only hurt myself by falling. That day, İsmail Ağa in Babybon was more respectful and polite toward me than necessary, unexpectedly refined for his hairy body. While I was sipping my beer, he came to me, "Boss, do you have any wishes or orders?" he said. "Not for now," I managed to say. Actually, every part of me was desire; that night, being alone, sleeping alone was death, the source of this feeling was neither lust nor horniness. My loneliness? I didn't know, I just wanted to take a prostitute from there and leave. I wanted to hug a prostitute and fall asleep. Since it was a weekday, the nightclub was empty; Central Anatolian folk songs had begun playing, and Romanian, Ukrainian, and Russian women were swaying to the rhythm. When an occasional popular pop song was played, all the women would flood the dance floor and start dancing together. This wasn't done for fun or pleasure. It was their job, an arrangement created for them to display themselves. The men in the nightclub could thus see all the women together and have the opportunity to choose. It was possible to see this as something disgusting, and some readers will think so. However, there, sitting at the bar, I would think this was very natural, even ingenious. What was being done here was no more disgusting or dishonorable than models who display themselves under the pretext of showcasing clothes on a catwalk. In fact, it was the same thing; there were just different levels of prostitution. This was a different level.

25

That day, because business was slow, the women had stayed on stage for 2-3 songs; it didn't matter to me. Any of them would do, any of them would be acceptable, but I had no money. Neither cash nor on my card... I had consumed everything. Taverns, bars, and nightclubs had eaten me up and finished me off. I was looking for a solution; I had to solve this, I shouldn't be alone that day either. İsmail Ağa was passing in front of me, busy. He always seemed to have work. As he passed, he gave a head nod in greeting, and I made a "come here" head gesture in response. He turned and came over, "Yes, boss?" he said. "İsmail Ağa, I've been coming and going for months, and you've been helpful in every way, today I really need it, help me out, send someone to my place, I'll pay you tomorrow," I said. İsmail Ağa laughed. "Boss, this business doesn't have credit; when it's 7-8 in the morning, the nightclub closes its accounts, there are no accounts left for the next day, if there are, it becomes a problem, the boss would make a fuss," he said. "I understand," I said, feeling helpless. "Look, Ağa, I've got an idea. You know my place is right over there; come look at the house, take whatever is useful to you, and send someone to me." This entire conversation was taking place around 2:00 AM. Ağa thought about it; this idea had appealed to him. "Boss, then you pay the bill, go home, and I'll be at your place in half an hour," he said. "Okay," I said, feeling happy and relieved.

26

I paid the bill, left, and went home. At home, I couldn't stay still; I kept looking from the balcony—from the balcony, Sadri Alışık Street was visible up to the point where it curved. It was the end of summer, the air was misty, and the nightclub lights were defining each mist particle one by one. Half an hour had passed, but İsmail Ağa wasn't visible; he hadn't come out yet, and I was starting to get anxious. The anxiety was sobering me up; my drunkenness was beginning to blend with the misty Istanbul air. "What if he doesn't come?" I was thinking. Another voice inside me was saying, "If he doesn't come, so what? What's the need for all this? Just lie down and crash!" As my head cleared, the nagging feeling of guilt inside me was becoming dominant. This feeling was so insidious that it was even reflected in my actions—I had turned off the few dim lights in the house and remained in complete darkness. In this darkness, no one could see me watching the street from the balcony. I was even ashamed in front of the prostitutes in the hotel across the street; I wanted the world not to know me, to forget me. Just as I was trying to make myself forgotten, to become invisible, I saw İsmail Ağa swinging his arms as he exited the nightclub's door. With a quickness unexpected from that body, he entered our building almost as soon as I saw him. I immediately ran to the apartment door and opened it. The apartment was on the third floor, and İsmail arrived breathless. He entered without permission. First, he looked around like a secondhand furniture dealer, then he began to look to me like a bailiff. "Boss, there's nothing useful here; everything's old," he said. No, I had made up my mind; this deal was going to happen. We walked around the house again. İsmail was just heading for the door when I said, "The television." "No, boss, I can't take that, that's going too far," he said. "No, no, take it, take it, there's no problem, I don't watch it anyway," I said. "Boss, you won't take it the wrong way, will you?" he said. "Yeah, I'm telling you to take it," I said. The television wasn't actually mine; it belonged to Ahmet, but I was going to give it away. I unplugged the TV's power and antenna, and İsmail came and hugged the television. "When will you send someone?" I asked as he hugged it. "Boss, it can't be very early today; this has become credit, I'll handle it out of my pocket, it'll take some time for me to gather the money. I'll put this in my back room; I was getting bored in the evenings," he said with a laugh as he left the house. I rushed to the balcony again, and a short while later, İsmail Ağa entered the nightclub carrying the large tube television. At three in the morning, I couldn't help but burst out laughing... The waiting period started again; I was beyond caring now, I would wait, if necessary, forever. I went inside, lay down, but couldn't sleep. Occasionally I would go out and look from the balcony. Then I went to the cupboard; there was one beer left from yesterday, I opened it, went back to the balcony, and started drinking. My stomach couldn't handle it, but I kept drinking. I couldn't win the battle with myself any other way. But it was only after five in the morning that the door rang; this was both good and bad. Good because the girl wouldn't be able to catch the service; the service was at six, they would return to their hotels by service in the mornings. Bad because I was exhausted from fatigue. I opened the door; a strange girl was smiling at me, wearing jeans and a red lace-embroidered shirt, as if she were from a village. I let her in; she entered with one leg limping, she was quite noticeably lame. After all that struggle and waiting all night, this was what arrived. A phrase immediately came to mind, and I couldn't help laughing. I turned to the girl, "Look, I'm going to teach you a saying, you wouldn't know it," I said. "In Turkey, they say 'unripe peach, lame woman's pussy,' just so you know," I said. I continued laughing. The girl didn't understand anything but was laughing. I realized she was Romanian, perhaps Gypsy, but she was a good person. We went to Tamer's old room; there was a floor mattress there. I don't remember most of it, but I suppose she was good in bed.

27

Around ten o'clock, I woke up in this decrepit house, which is the last stop on Sadri Alışık Street, or the first stop of Turnacıbaşı. According to address records, it's in Turnacıbaşı, but this building faces Sadri Alışık, so it's in a neither-here-nor-there situation. I tried to describe the street, but the house is another world. Under this building, there's a secondhand shop. A kind of antique dealer, buying and selling old things. This shop and the building entrance are so intermingled that you can't tell whether you're entering the shop or the building. This old furniture smell starts from the entrance and would permeate the entire stairwell up to the third floor where our apartment was. This smell, unable to stop, would enter the house and mix with the old smell of the house. The stairs were wide and wooden, covered with carpet, and fastened with brass rods in the front to prevent the carpet from slipping. There was one apartment on each floor. Our apartment had never been renovated, and everything was in its natural state. High wooden doors, wooden parquet floors, woodwork, even the bathroom. First, you would enter a hall; in the hall, on the right was a room, which was my room; right next to the entrance was a bathroom; on the left, a small kitchen; and across, a double door, through which you entered the living room. The living room faced Turnacıbaşı, and a bay window balcony directly faced Sadri Alışık. In one corner of the living room, a high-glassed, white, two-winged wooden door separated an area. A separate room had been established here. In the early days, until he left, Tamer had stayed here; after he left, we had made this the guest room, with only a carpet and a floor mattress. Since the woodwork in my room faced north, it had really rotted; I would sometimes sleep there on cold nights or when I came home with another woman—besides Ela—I would sleep there. This was just a method to alleviate my feeling of guilt. That morning, when I woke up in this room, the Romanian girl Marina, with one lame leg, was still lying beside me. This situation was very strange; these girls never sleep, no matter what time it is, no matter how tired they are, they would leave, but Marina had stayed. She was wearing one of my white shirts. I got up, brushed my teeth, and washed my face, then checked my pockets, wallet, and phone. Everything was intact; only the television was missing from the house. When I came back to the room, Marina was still sleeping. She was lying on her side with one leg pulled up toward her stomach; she was wearing a light green, tulle-like underwear, and the white shirt had ridden up. I didn't remember much of the evening, but I was thinking in a utilitarian and pragmatic way: the television was gone, and the girl had stayed here. I lay down next to Marina, pulled her green underwear down, put her leg back in place, gently pressed on her body, and laid her face down. "Hmm, nu nu nu," she was making sounds like this, but I had already completely removed her green underwear and had gently slipped inside her from behind, while she was saying "nu nu nu." The "nu" sounds had stopped and turned into moans; I was going back and forth, then I slightly rose from her, held her hips from underneath, and lifted them. She had risen on her knees on the bed; I entered her again. Marina was also losing herself. We made love for a long time; my favorite lovemaking was in the mornings when hungover... When I returned from the shower, Marina was sitting cross-legged on the floor mattress and had lit a cigarette. We had probably exchanged a total of ten words since the night before. For the first time, I looked carefully at her face. Her face was pure white, her eyes black, her hair black and at her shoulders. She had applied bright red lipstick to her lips while I was in the shower, and with each puff of her cigarette, the cigarette became even redder. Marina was constantly smiling, as if she were afraid I would get angry or upset with her if she didn't smile. I had lain down next to her on the floor mattress again. I was looking at her back. "Shall we have breakfast?" I said; she turned to me with a smile. Then she put out her cigarette and got up, went to the shower. When she returned, she was wearing her own red shirt—so she must have taken it off in the living room at night—then she took her jeans and put them on. She stood up and looked at me, with a strange accent, she said, "I should go now." I got up and said, "Okay." She took her gray fabric jacket from the armchair. I hadn't noticed this jacket at all during the night. I went with Marina to the door. She smiled again, kissed me on the cheek, and left...

28

After Marina left, I remained sitting in the armchair in the living room. The upholstery of the two armchairs was worn, with corner stitches coming undone in places. The color of the fabric was indistinguishable; there were green patterns on beige. Or perhaps the armchairs were burgundy, with yellow patterns; aging had made the colors indefinable. Besides the two armchairs, there was also a loveseat. It was newer, more modern. Its frame was soft, as were the armrests; it was a comfortable sofa with ideal supporting angles for making love. Across from the loveseat was a console table on which the television had stood, but now that was gone too. Its surface was covered with small souvenirs, trinkets, figurines, and boxes that Ahmet had collected over the years. Another beautiful aspect of this house was the books. The large bookcase was in the room where I slept, a room that was quite gloomy and depressing even during the day. Its window faced the sea side, toward Çukurcuma, with a melancholy view that showed the roofs of buildings but couldn't see the sea. The window frames were beyond repair and would whistle according to the direction and speed of the wind. We would try to heat this room with an electric heater. There was no kitchen door; the kitchen was like a niche integrated with the entrance hall, narrow and small, but cooking was possible. The six-person dining table in the living room had taken on the duty of collecting clutter. Everyone who came would drop their bag, tote, or book on this table. On weekends or holidays, I would declare a house-cleaning mobilization. I wanted the surface of this table to be completely empty because this table would transform into my work table. I would brew my tea, sit at the table, borrow one of Ahmet's antique notebooks collected over the years, and start writing. The balcony door was always open; I needed the outside sounds for writing. I would feel very special, very bohemian, very lonely, very intellectual, and I would derive a separate pleasure from all these feelings during these times. I included some of these writings in the first book; if you've read the first book and moved on to this second book, you will have read these texts—you can figure out which ones they are.

29

While I was in this contradictory state of mind, where was Ela? As the question mark in my head grew larger, memories of the moments Ela and I had experienced in this house came to my mind. She had left me again, forgetting our days in the house. Ela would leave without reason, without timing. She had left every concept related to togetherness naked on the table and gone. Love, passion, habit, sex, sexuality, sadism-masochism, affection—all of them, if you can think of them—without looking back. And I was just waiting, though not a faithful wait according to some... I too had squeezed my own concepts into a corner of the table.

I was glad to have met Marina. She was someone completely opposite to Ela, in my view. She didn't make love in a closed way like Ela; she was out in the open with everything. She was embarrassed by words, not by sex. Marina had passed through the night without reminding me of Ela's absence. Would I ever see Marina again, or had she too run away from me? I was full of anxieties; did I have the strength to tidy up the house? The morning lovemaking had sobered me up; there wasn't the severe hangover that had been mentioned. The messiness of the room didn't bother me at all. Now, while everything was so messy, it was necessary to go out. I got ready quickly and went down the stairs without slowing down.

30

I'm trying to tell this story through the street, excavating memories from the depths of my mind; my brain hurts, it bleeds as I dig... My memory is giving birth to its past, and I am telling it!

Across from the apartment entrance is the street. On one side is the hotel where prostitutes sleep. The building across from it is in need of renovation. The building was crying, shouting "Help, oh messenger of God!" There was no one to hear its voice! It was confiding its troubles to me every time I went out on the street. Perhaps I alone saw and knew and understood the tears flowing from its eaves. For some reason, they were painting it a jarring blue! The building was complaining, it didn't want this, it was vomiting the paint. They had set up the scaffolding and kept applying more and more paint, applying it to its aching skin as it threw up the thinner and paint...

If you leave our building and turn left, heading upward, Turnacıbaşı takes you and carries you to Galatasaray. If you turn right and let yourself go downward, you'll reach Çukurcuma and Cihangir. Turnacıbaşı, in this state, is a long Pythagorean hypotenuse, a ray that pierces through Beyoğlu. To understand the structure of Istanbul's streets in this area, you need to think in quantum terms. That is, if New York was built according to the laws of Newtonian physics, Istanbul operates with quantum physics. Straight logic won't get you to the address you want here. There is no flatness, no grid plan; hills and slopes dominate the organism. Only if you align your mind with these rules will you find the paths, otherwise you'll get lost. Of course, there are parallel streets too, but their continuity is short and deceptive. If you want to escape the tiresome crowd of İstiklal Street and are looking for an above-ground tunnel, Turnacıbaşı is always ready to take you from our house to Galatasaray. This street, with its gentle slope, doesn't tire you; it's quiet and calm. However, if a vehicle escapes from Galatasaray and enters this street, and encounters a vehicle coming from the opposite direction, the festivities begin, and the cars turn into goats on a bridge...

31

From the house coordinates to Galatasaray Hamam, for a long time, there wasn't any place I frequented on this street. Then I discovered a small shop. Two tables, four chairs, a little eatery... The back of the shop was divided by a curtain, with a two-eyed stove and an old man with a bent back making pot dishes on a small gas cylinder flame. His food might not have been as good and tasty as other eateries, but it was always calm, always shaded, like being under a tree. In the other eatery, everyone was crammed together, in a hurry to eat quickly and leave. Here there was no rush. There was a languid slowness that intoxicated people. It had Istanbul's most delicious, spiciest pickled peppers. This spiciness went with every meal. There was another eatery at the bottom of the building across the street. We called it a "yemekçi" (food place) because it wasn't a restaurant, wasn't a "lokanta," wasn't a soup kitchen, café, or fixed-menu place—it was a "yemekçi," opening at 11:30 in the morning and closing at 15:00 in the afternoon, serving only lunch. The cooks would come early in the morning, and the food would be cooked until room was made by the yemekçi's cooks. There would be 4-5 types of dishes, 6-7 tables, and during the 3 hours it was open, it would fill and empty perhaps 5 times. When the food started to run out, everyone knew it was about to close; food never went to waste at the yemekçi, it was sold and eaten completely. It was a delicious meal for those working in the area who didn't have much money; the main dish was a home-style meal, neither with too little meat nor too much salt, the yemekçi didn't cheat you, it had unlimited bread, spicy pickled peppers. Its best, most favorite dish for me was the stew and rice; the dried dish was fantastic, in summer the moussaka, stew, stuffed vegetables, stuffed vine leaves, with yogurt on the side, available in every season with every meal... We would fill our stomachs at the yemekçi...

Galatasaray Hamam was at the outer corner of the corner, and at the inner corner was a small antique shop, a shop where I never bought anything but always looked through the window. From this corner, Turnacıbaşı turned sharply, almost ninety degrees, and once it turned, its face opened to another world. Now İstiklal flowed into it. These were the measurements within İstiklal's reach.

32

Before reaching İstiklal Avenue, a narrow street branches off to the left, a kind of last exit before the bridge-type escape. This street is important and very narrow. At the exact inner corner, there's a place half below ground level. This is one of those places in Beyoğlu that constantly changes owners, unable to find its identity. It's the neighborhood's non-existent, unviable establishment. Entering the street and proceeding a bit, there's a bar on the right called Urban. It's an intellectual, respectable place. It will have a separate place in this story. It's in this mentioned establishment that I encounter Deniz unexpectedly. Deniz was a female friend I knew from

Ankara. We had met in one of the bar scenes. We liked each other.

I'll continue my story with Deniz later; the street is calling me now...

The other importance of the street, like the narrow arm of Turnacıbaşı, is that it continues the hypotenuse shortcut. The street eventually turns right and leads directly and steeply to İstiklal. Cross İstiklal without waiting and you'll enter the street of the fish market. Now you can breathe a sigh of relief because you're in another world. Thus, knowing this shortcut, being able to go from home to the fish market without walking on İstiklal, without flowing in the crowd, is a good opportunity.

I entered the fish market street exactly as described. I didn't know the name of this street—Now I've learned that it's called Sahne Street. A good name; many things were staged here. It fit well.—I don't know why I entered this street, a habit, an involuntariness, a reflection. I entered, found myself on the street. I looked around; the crowd was always the same crowd. There was a homogeneous distribution for every hour, a certain proportion of women, men, tourists, young, old... It had been planned this way.

33

I looked at my watch; it was four in the afternoon. What should I do? If I had Ela on one side and Marina on the other, sitting in a tavern in Nevizade, opening a large rakı, them telling stories and me crying, me telling stories and them crying... Marina might start a story, how her leg became crippled, how and why she fled from Bucharest? How she fell into Istanbul, into Babybon? But if there were no language between us, understanding each other easily, in what language I don't know... Then Ela might take the saz in her hand, explain why she ran away from me, present her intellectual, enlightened justifications to me. Womanly, somewhat feminist, but anarchist justifications. I might become emotional; we might discover our common points, the three of us, a triple love against this society, a daring love, a respectable, courageous love... Taking back respectability, a disgraceful and brave love... Then I might explain my reasons, why I drink, why I plan to destroy myself (self-destruction, self-demolition, self-detonation), why I see life as a long suicide? I might present my dialectical proofs. I might draw a diagram on napkins, we would all examine it together. Then, Marina might confess that she was actually born in a village in Bucharest. "I knew it," I would say, we would hold hands, when one holds one hand and the other holds my other hand, I wouldn't be able to drink my rakı, I would get annoyed. Marina wouldn't be able to stand it, she would make me drink with her own hands. Ela would put her hand on my neck, I would burst out laughing. I would unbutton my shirt down to my belly, again bursting out laughing. (Then I look, and there's another scene in front of me. I see myself as İsmail Ağa. We're at Babybon. Ela stands on one side with an awkward makeup on her face. Marina's back is bare, in a yellow dress, with a red carnation in her hair. Ela has roses blooming on her head. I'm wearing clothes that don't belong to me, a grey, shiny striped suit. Babybon has become another place, we're no longer at Babybon, we're at a wedding venue. We've set up tables under the trees, strung wires from tree to tree, hung light bulbs. I take a sip from my rakı, occasionally I get up and fire the fourteen-shot pistol in my belt into the air. Both Ela and Marina are happy. I am the man, I am İsmail Ağa...) When I wake up from this nightmare, I find myself in front of İmroz. I don't go in. I shouldn't go in; there's no point in going in. I need to gather my thoughts, organize what I'm going to do. I go to the beerhouse next to İmroz and sit down, order a beer. When it comes, I take a few sips without waiting; now I feel better. I take my small black notebook out of my pocket; only by taking notes can I understand myself and what's happening.

34

(How I perceived myself: I had collapsed, spinning in a vicious circle. More like a triangle, with one corner of the triangle at Galatasaray, which connects to the fish market, Nevizade, and surroundings forming a separate rectangle. The second point is where Sadri Alışık and İstiklal intersect, the Ağa Mosque point; the third point is home. I couldn't escape this triangle, as if time had frozen, as if time had stopped and I was moving independently of time.)

35

It was a long holiday period, and the best part of working at the consulate was that it was impossible to work during official holidays. The work was also a mess. The truth is, I needed to work, to not lose the job, and why hadn't I gone back to Ankara! Because of Ela, but she wasn't there; I kept sinking as I turned back. I had created my own mud, my own swamp.

Black Notebook:

1. **Ela** / not my girlfriend-lover-fiancée, but could be / age 26

I love her, but how?

Very smart, intelligent, and intellectual

Our tastes align.

In bed we are mediocre. Shy, I'm the first man she's slept with. Before meeting me, she had problems with men. She could only be with me / an attractive person / height 172, weight 48, model measurements, very thin, but sexy! Black hair, very fine hair strands, dark-skinned, but not too dark. Her kissing is very beautiful, sincere, and warm. I enjoy drinking with her.

2. Marina / age 22-23 / Romanian national / prostitute-hostess / one leg limps.

Works at Babybon.

Do I love her? No. Why am I interested? A bit of pity, mercy, loneliness.

But she's very beautiful, so what if one leg is short, height over 175, white skin, firm and full buttocks, firm breasts.

She's very good in bed. The main reason is my search for pornographic imagery, physical satisfaction.

3. Deniz / My friend from Ankara. Short, red-haired, with large, huge breasts, a sweet person. We meet occasionally at Urban, we run into each other, we drink beer. She wants to move in with me, but just as a friend; my house is good and nice, but very cold; winter is coming. The woodwork lets in drafts, we're checking. Problem: I can't be friends with women; if we're in the same house, I might want to sleep with her. In fact, I already want to sleep with her, for no reason, just a manly thing... But I don't think she wants to sleep with me; this is a problem.
4. Me / I know myself; there is a self within me, many selves have entered me, I'm trying to extract them, to explain them to you.

Practical, utilitarian, current problems: I need to find money, I need to go to Babybon tonight, I need to see Marina.

36

I finish my beer and get up, walking up Balo Street toward İstiklal. When I reach İstiklal, I stop, considering my options: using the large hypotenuse to go home, using the small hypotenuse to go home, going home via İstiklal, going to Urban, or going to Bahadır by the same routes. (Bahadır is my friend from high school, living in Çukurcuma, one street below mine; I'm thinking of going to borrow money from him.) İstiklal's time has come. I start walking toward Taksim. I remember this story.

I walked on the right, and after just a few steps, I entered Atlas; there was a bar under this cinema. Deniz would sometimes hang out here, but she wasn't here today. The bar was empty, its air perfectly clean; I wanted to sit and have a beer, but my head was spinning from just one beer. Had the evening exploded, or was it the beer? I didn't know. I left and continued along İstiklal. When I reached Ağa Mosque, I stopped, looked, and asked, "What part of you is a mosque?" It heard me, looked, but couldn't answer. Then I heard a voice; it was speaking from the windows in its wall, saying, "What part of you are you, what part of you are you?" Just as I was entering Sadri Alışık Street, I turned back, went up to the mosque wall, and looked inside through the windows in the wall. It looked peaceful, silent; on one side of me, people were flowing on İstiklal. I didn't enter the mosque. "What part of me, huh? We'll see," I said, entering the street and walking quickly toward home...

37

The street was lively. The owner of the antique shop, who was also our landlord, had put two armchairs outside and was chatting with someone. There was a kiosk under the house; the kiosk owner was like a kind of neighborhood headman. Who came, who went, leave a key, take it—all this was his business, as was buying beer on credit. Before entering the house, I wanted to buy two beers, so I stopped by. "I'll pay for them tomorrow," I said and took them. "Oh, by the way, Tamer came by and asked for you," said the kiosk owner. Where had this Tamer come from now? I went up to the house, opened my beer, and started sipping it in the armchair, but it wasn't going down. I was stuck. I was looking at the faded colors of the house; everything was faded, colors drained. I thought about my own old age—my color would drain and fade like this—but this didn't frighten me. Even now, I didn't feel bright and young. In fact, I found aging, old age, and elderliness beautiful; it had its own aesthetic, but only those who could endure understood this. The paint on the walls was peeling off in shells, then mixing with the dust on the floor and escaping to the corners of the rooms. The coverings of the doors had separated from the glue holding them, and they too hung like dry tree bark where they were. I too was hanging where I was. There were so many people in my life, but none of them were here. Why weren't they here? Why wasn't I calling Ela? Why wasn't she calling me? What if I went across to Göztepe and stayed at her house? Last holiday, when her parents went to their hometown, she had taken me home. How beautiful it was to sleep in Ela's bed, in her room, to be close to her, to share a woman's room, to browse among her books, to read the poems she read, to touch the books she touched, to listen to the cassettes she listened to. I probably loved her, even loved her madly, and she loved me too, was jealously crazy about me, but the urge to suffer was pushing us away from each other. Like the repulsion of like poles. If we were to converge, to be as close as we desired and longed for, there would be a nuclear explosion, we would transition to a quantum universe... We didn't have the strength to be that close. —My love, I miss you. Remember how I stayed at my aunt's in Selami Çeşme for you, we would meet every night at a bar on the street, a bar without air or windows. I miss those days too, come now... Don't make me wander this Beyoğlu; this loneliness adds to my lostness. Look, I'm fading like this house; I'm running away from myself...

I waited!

There was neither a comer nor a goer...

I threw myself outside.

38
The street had come alive. Laughing, shouting, and teasing, a group of Romani girls passed by. I had no idea what they were doing here or why they were in this part of town. One of them was strikingly beautiful. She wore a brightly colored skirt, a smoky-gray patterned blouse, and over that, a wrinkled white shirt. The shirt's right sleeve had slipped off her shoulder. The collar of her blouse was worn out and sagging from too many washes. As she moved, her chest would reveal itself and then vanish again, like a fleeting secret.

On her feet were low-heeled, floppy slippers that made a slapping sound with every step. They were clearly too small, with half her heel hanging out, forcing her to walk partially on her toes. You could almost count each bone in her foot. Her veins swelled and receded like an anatomical specimen, her legs tensing and relaxing rhythmically. She was dark-skinned—though not in any definable way—one of the thousand shades of brown: part coal, part ash, and a hint of crimson.

Her legs were long, unnaturally long by ordinary human proportions. But what stood out most were her hips. They tilted sharply upward, as if they alone straightened her entire body, lifting her like wings. It was a vertical walk, almost defiant. With every step, she seemed to rise, as if trying to pierce the air and carve a violet rupture in the atmosphere.

Every time she passed in front of me, I froze, unable to tear my eyes away from her hips. And every time she saw me, she would whip her long hair around and flash a wild, unrestrained smile before darting away. Her teeth were dazzling white, big and strong like a horse's. There was something animalistic in her beauty—raw, magnetic, impossible to ignore.

After she disappeared down the street, I turned right from where I'd been standing by the door and began walking. I was heading down to Çukurcuma to stop by Bahadır's place and ask him for a loan. I had just passed the corner kiosk when the vendor shouted after me, "Hey man, Tamer was here—you know that, right?"

He had stepped out of the kiosk, lit a long Marlboro, one hand on his waist, hiding the cigarette behind his back for some reason. I turned around and nodded to show I knew, then walked on quickly. Why did he keep bringing this up? He knew I didn't like Tamer. The guy had made my life hell during those early weeks. And yet, every time I tried to avoid even hearing his name, the kiosk guy would still say it:

"Hey man, Tamer was here."

39

The hypotenuse of Turnacıbaşı Street didn't end at our place—it went on a bit further. Just past our building, under the one next door, stood the historic Ağa Hamamı. Truth be told, during the entire year or so I lived in this neighborhood, I never once visited the bath. Well, I did step inside once—but not to bathe. I was completely drunk, mistook it for our house, and stumbled in fully clothed all the way to the central marble platform. After that, I never had the face to go back.

The end of Turnacıbaşı was another 40 or 50 meters downhill from our house. At that point, the street curved to the right and became something else, with a new name, a new identity. There were other ways to go, of course—if you wanted to head toward Sıraselviler, two separate roads, each at a different incline, would take you to different spots along it. But if you turned right and followed what was now Ağa Hamamı Street, you could reach Çukurcuma, or even go farther and end up in Cihangir.

I was on my way to Çukurcuma, to visit Bahadır. I took the first right off Ağa Hamamı Street—that was Yadigâr Street. This street will have a special place later in the story. Yadigâr Street was short—not even 50 meters long—and charming. It was one of the first streets in Çukurcuma to come alive with antique shops and art galleries. At its end, the road curved left and sloped gently toward the sea, becoming yet another street.

Bahadır's apartment was in the building just to the left at the corner. In terms of pure geometry, his place sat directly behind ours—I could see it from my bedroom window. But since there was no direct passage, I had to make a full U-shaped detour, circling around three streets to reach it.

After all that, I stood downstairs and rang Bahadır's bell for a long time. No answer. I tried again. And again. For about fifteen minutes I kept at it, then finally started shouting, "Bahadırrrr! Bahadırrr!"
Once it became clear he wasn't home, I sat down at the edge of the wall on the corner and waited a while. No one came.

There was nothing else to do. With the bitterness of someone who couldn't reach his destination, I turned back the way I came—Yadigâr to Ağa Hamamı, and back up Turnacıbaşı. As I neared our house, I crossed the street just to avoid the kiosk guy, then quickly turned onto Sadri Alışık.

Babybon was still asleep. The other bar door was open, and Dire Straits was playing inside. Bonbon was asleep too. I climbed the hill with all my strength, moving fast. I had almost no money left, it was nearly evening, and I hadn't eaten a thing all day. I hadn't felt the hunger because I was still hungover, but now my stomach had begun to rebel—burning, bitter, aching—pleading for something, anything, to soothe it.

I started cursing at Bahadır in a kind of friendly fury. "Asshole, pimp, wouldn't even piss on a wounded finger... not that he ever pissed on anything, anyway," I muttered to myself.

If I had any money in my pocket, I would've taken the next turn, sat down at Mutlu Ocakbaşı, ordered a liver skewer, followed by an Adana kebab. A small bottle of rakı, some turnip juice, a bowl of strained yogurt with cucumbers, a plate of spicy ezme... I would've indulged, let it all go. My head and my stomach would've celebrated together. But I had nothing—I'd blown all my cash at the nightclub. Now I was broke, starving, and stranded.

When I reached İstiklal, I didn't even glance at the Ağa Mosque. I was afraid it might speak—say something heavy. What would I say back? "What part of you is a mosque?" again?
I was ashamed. I kept walking fast, toward Galatasaray. I didn't want to run into anyone I knew. I had no hope in anyone anymore. It felt like the whole world had made a pact to abandon and erase me.
They couldn't care less.

I was helpless. I was pathetic.

And Marina? I had to find her. But how could I, with nothing in my pocket?
And Ela? Why did she turn her back on me—was it just to watch me go through this?
I didn't know.

All I wanted now was a meal. I couldn't even think straight anymore. Hunger, a hangover, depression—it all blurred together. I had stopped being able to think.

40

Just before reaching Çiçek Pasajı, I stopped in front of a shoe shop. First, I stared blankly at the shoes, then gathered all the coins and bills from my jeans and jacket pockets into the right pocket of my coat. I checked every slot in my wallet and found a forgotten ten million lira bill. I was thrilled. I added it—and the rest of the coins—into the same pocket. Yes, I now had enough money to drink two Tekel beers at the beerhouse inside Çiçek Pasajı, maybe even a little left over. My face lit up with a sudden smile.

I hurried into Çiçek Pasajı. The beerhouse was set apart from the arcade by a wooden glass partition, sitting on the left like it had been dropped in from another world. The walls were decorated with quotes about the benefits of beer. I ordered a draft Tekel—payment was upfront, so I paid. This tiny place didn't have seating; everyone stood as they drank. They didn't serve food, but bringing your own snacks wasn't forbidden.

Next to me stood a short, wrinkled old man carefully balancing salted peanuts from a small paper pouch with sips of his beer. I wasn't nearly as composed—I'd nearly downed half my beer in the first gulp. My goal was to get my head buzzing as quickly as possible, to shake off this lost and weary mood. But one beer wasn't going to do it. I finished the rest in just two gulps and rushed back outside.

I entered Çiçek Pasajı itself. The tables were slowly filling up, the sky was darkening—my favorite time of day, the best time to start drinking. But I couldn't really start. I walked slowly through the passage, eyeing the meze on the tables. Head waiters invited me over, but I was a hopeless customer—they could see it in my eyes.

When I reached Balık Pazarı Street, I turned toward İstiklal instead of heading to Nevizade. That would've only tortured me more. I stepped into Şampiyon Kokoreç. I had just enough for a quarter sandwich and one more beer. I ordered the quarter kokoreç, counted my money, and asked the price of a single skewer of fried mussels. Yes—it would be just enough.
"Chief, throw a single mussel skewer into the sandwich," I said.
That would make it more filling, and the mussel–kokoreç combo was delicious.

They wrapped it in parchment paper. I paid and went back inside to load it up—generous red pepper and plenty of lemon squeezed between the bread. My mouth was craving sharp, aggressive flavors.

I ran back to the small beer shop at the entrance of Çiçek and ordered another Tekel. As soon as it arrived, I paid for it. That was it—I had zero money left. The balance sheet read zero to zero.

Now, I was trying to balance my quarter sandwich with my beer—careful not to run out of one before the other, alternating precise bites and measured sips. The old alcoholics around me were doing the same. Their hands shook as they raised their beers, taking a sip before returning to their peanuts or, like me, their bread.

I felt alright here—but once it was over, I would have to leave. If only I had more money, I'd get a half kokoreç with a full skewer of mussels, two more beers on the side, and I'd be myself again. But I didn't...

At last, I managed to finish my beer and the sandwich at almost the exact same moment. As soon as they were gone, I threw myself back out into the street—back to İstiklal.

41
I had no choice but to go home. As soon as I arrived, I threw myself onto the two-seater couch. Without bothering to undress or freshen up, I started flipping through the poetry book Ahmet had gifted me—Cemal Süreya's collected works—but I couldn't really read it. Even if I did, I couldn't understand a word. My eyes drifted across the lines, unable to make any sense or form any unity. I was still hungover, and the three beers I'd had during the day had turned my head into a sponge. My neck was numb, and a heavy headache throbbed at my temples. I kept squinting.

Those last two beers and the quarter sandwich had only made my hunger worse. They hadn't helped at all. I closed the book, but didn't put it down. It rested in my hand. Then I looked at the front cover: *Love Poems*. I murmured under my breath—"Love poems... love poems..."
Should I try to write a poem in this state? I wondered.
No, no...

I flipped back to the beginning. On the first blank page, in Ahmet's careful, architect's handwriting, he had written at the top:

ISTANBUL 1997

I closed the book again. Ahmet came to mind. Why hadn't I called him? He was my boss. And isn't that what bosses are for? For times like these. I was staying in miserable conditions and still doing his work. Besides, with Ahmet, you never knew—maybe he'd come to Istanbul, picked up one or two flings, and was already sitting in Imroz, ordering rakı and seafood. The moment he heard my voice, he'd say:
"Come right away."
And fifteen minutes later, I'd be seated at the table.

I grabbed the phone and dialed. It rang and rang—finally, he picked up:

"Hey man, how are you?"
"Good, you?"
"Not bad. I'm in Istanbul, you know. Didn't go to Ankara. Are you around here?"
"Yeah, yeah, I know—you're holding down the shop. Hah! How's it going?"
"Not bad, really, but I'm a bit tight on cash. You know, with the holiday and all, I didn't get my salary. I gave all the work advances to the guys going back to their hometowns. The banks are closed. Just thought I'd check if you were in town."
"Hmm... Well, I'm not in Istanbul. I came to Antalya to

see my brother. But hey—remember Taner? He owed me some money. He dropped by the house while I was gone. Since he couldn't find you, he left the money with the kiosk guy. Go pick it up and count it as a work advance."

42

It finally clicked. Now I understood why the kiosk guy kept saying, "Hey man, Tamer stopped by." That was it—he had dropped off the money. But the guy hadn't mentioned the cash. If I hadn't asked, he probably would've used it himself during the holiday—maybe spent it at the Tekel shop.

I thanked Ahmet and hung up. Without even putting on my jacket, I stepped on the heels of my shoes and darted outside. I had to grab the money before the kiosk guy left. At a certain hour, he always handed the kiosk over to his brother—and his brother probably didn't know anything about the envelope. I'd end up out of luck again.

Out of breath, I poked my head through the kiosk window. The guy looked at me with an indifferent expression.
"What's up, man?" he said.
"Tamer stopped by!"
"Yeah, man, I've told you twice already—Tamer came by."
"Okay, fine, he came by—but why didn't you tell me about the money, man?"
"Well, I figured you already knew. I was just reminding you. But then you stormed off and I didn't get a chance to say anything."
"Alright, alright—just give me the money."

The cash was in a narrow white envelope. I paid him back for the two beers I'd had earlier that day, slid the envelope into my pocket, and headed back up to the apartment. As I climbed the stairs, I was muttering calm, composed curses at the kiosk guy.

At home, I counted the money. It was good money—enough to get me through the holiday, as long as I didn't do anything stupid. Of course, there was still the matter of getting the TV back—or maybe buying a new one and cooking up some excuse for Ahmet. A new one would be better anyway. İsmail Ağa would want fresh money for that piece of junk.

I cleaned up, shaved, changed clothes. First order of business was to fill my stomach—then I'd figure out the rest. I'd go to Babybon later in the evening. I didn't know exactly what I'd do there, but I'd think about that afterward.

I left some of the money at home and stepped outside. I decided to head to Umut Ocakbaşı. It was cheap, filling, and close by. And they had rakı and şalgam too. All the essentials.

I was climbing the Sadri Alışık hill with a newfound confidence—strutting a little, glancing around with a look of casual disdain. Babybon hadn't opened yet; I'd see them in the evening. The other bar had flung its doors wide open to air the place out. Inside, The Doors were playing. A few rookie drinkers had already taken their spots, nursing their beers. Bonbon was still closed—maybe someone was getting things ready inside—but the iron door at the short flight of stairs was still shut.

Using my hands on my hips for extra leverage, I climbed the slope. The street where Umut Ocakbaşı was located was the last one on the right before reaching İstiklal. Not many streets branched off from Sadri Alışık—this one felt like an escape route, but it had its own kind of character.

Back then, the area had a few folk bars and a couple of shabby dives. Umut Ocakbaşı was just beginning to gain popularity—a place known only to those in the know. The place was scrappy, and that scrappiness had become the latest trend among newly minted intellectuals trying to appear edgy. What mattered to me was that it was cheap, and the food had a sweet, rich flavor.

After Umut Ocakbaşı, the street had a few secondhand bookshops, and beyond that, another narrow, short street began.

43

When I entered the grillhouse, I went straight upstairs—the ground floor was already full. The early diners always came here first, because after a certain hour, the liver skewers ran out. They made only a limited number. If you wanted liver, you had to be early. I liked eating early, liver or no liver.

The upper floor was made up of small rooms connected to one another, but in the largest room, right in the center, was a grill. There was also one downstairs. The tables and chairs were wooden, and the tables were covered with yellow parchment paper that was constantly being replaced.

They seated me at a table near the corner, where I could still see the grill. That mattered—seeing the grill was important. Eye contact with the cook standing at the fire had a particular seriousness to it.

The table had just been vacated, and the paper was already stained—drops of reddish grease scattered across it, somewhere between crimson and maroon. Parsley and salad crumbs were scattered here and there, and in one or two spots, traces of yogurt from cacık still lingered. I was impatient for someone to come and change the paper. I sat carefully, trying not to touch the table, feeling like a guest in someone else's messy home.

A young guy arrived first, a bundle of parchment sheets hanging from his forearm. He hung them over the back of the chair across from me, then expertly folded up the old paper—crumbs and all—and, with two swift pulls from his bundle, laid a fresh layer across the table. All of it took just seconds. He never looked at me. As he turned to leave, I said,
"Can I order now?"
"Boss will be here in a sec," he replied, already scooping up dishes from the next table and tossing my used paper onto the stack. He balanced it all in his hands, adjusting to the awkward weight, and shuffled away toward the stairs with short, hurried steps.

Now I could rest my elbows on the clean parchment, let my hands spread out across its smooth surface. It gave me a sense of clarity—of cleansing. I felt calmer.

Finally, the head waiter arrived, and he didn't come empty-handed. Without even looking at me, he set down a plate of greens, a bowl of strained yogurt with cucumbers, and a spicy ezme. Then he straightened up and looked me in the eye.
"What can I get you, brother?"
"Liver," I said.

Without delay, he turned to the cook behind the grill and shouted, "One liver!"
The cook acknowledged with a quick nod. Clearly, the liver was in demand—only a few remained.

"What'll you have after the liver?" the waiter asked.
"We'll see," I said. "Probably Adana next. I'll let you know. But get that liver started right away."
"You got it."
He turned back to the grill. "Liver, urgent!" he called out.

He was rotating between me and the cook with smooth, practiced moves.
"What'll you drink?" he asked.
"A small rakı and a şalgam," I said—and even just saying it lifted my spirits. A strange joy bloomed inside me.

He had turned away when I added, "Make sure the şalgam is spicy," with emphasis.

No sooner had he gone than the busboy arrived with the drinks. The şalgam was served in empty rakı or glass water bottles—brought in from Adana in big jugs and poured into these reused bottles. He set down a small bottle of rakı, the şalgam, and two aluminum-capped water bottles on my table and left.

As he walked away, I called after him,
"Hey kid, bring me plenty of lemon."
"Right away, brother!" he replied, gesturing rapidly in acknowledgement.

On the table were two rakı glasses turned upside down. With my right hand, I gave them a practiced twist and sat them upright on my end of the table. The wet rings they left behind looked like a pair of eyes staring up at me. The paper was so thin, it was nearly soaked through.

I poured my rakı carefully, somewhere between a single and a double. Everything was still cold—no need for ice in the first few rounds. Later, once things softened up, ice would become essential. I poured water into the second glass. Rakı without water was unthinkable—but I had no glass left for the şalgam.

I looked around for the busboy. He'd vanished. The head waiter was nowhere in sight either. Oh well, I'd drink the first sip without the şalgam.

I raised the rakı glass to my lips, touched it lightly like a small kiss, then tilted it slowly. Without pausing, I let a third of it slide down my throat and into my stomach. I followed it with a sip of water, dipped my fork into the cacık, and popped a small bite into my mouth.

A puckered expression of satisfaction spread across my face—topped with a faint smile.

Suddenly, the busboy reappeared, scurrying around again.
"Hey kid, can I get another glass?" I asked.
Without missing a beat, he snatched a pair of glasses from a newly set table and placed them exactly over the fading wet marks on my parchment. Apparently, these glasses always came in pairs—inseparable twins.

I filled one of them with şalgam. Now, before my right hand stood a neat formation: rakı, water, and şalgam—lined up like soldiers, all in matching rakı glasses. I felt protected, fortified.

I took my second sip of rakı—this time chasing it with the spicy şalgam. That şalgam—it was a rakı traitor, really. You could drink rakı forever without a single meze if you had that stuff. But it had a side effect: it stoked hunger. Fiercely.

Now the hunger hit me hard. Where the hell was that liver?

I couldn't wait anymore. The rakı and şalgam had awakened a digestion beast inside me—a fire-breathing dragon tearing through my belly. My anticipation had become visible—so much so that even the head waiter and the cook had noticed. The waiter gave a subtle signal to the cook, urging him to move my plate to the front of the queue.

That was a good sign.

44
Thank God, in the meantime, the busboy had come by and left a metal plate piled with triangular pieces of lavash. Back in my hometown, we'd call it flatbread or yufka, but here they called it lavash—it didn't matter to me. It was just bread you could wrap and eat. The tips of the pieces were thicker with dough, still dusted with flour. I grabbed one triangle and immediately started eating, combining it with the ezme, cacık, and greens in front of me. Between bites, I took sips of rakı and şalgam, devouring everything with great appetite.

A small voice in the back of my mind said, *"Slow down— leave room for the meat,"* but my hunger knew no brakes. Thankfully, I had just finished my first round of rakı and had paused to prepare the second when the liver skewers finally arrived.

"Careful, they're hot!" the waiter said as he placed them down. But I ignored the warning—before the words even registered, I had already grabbed one of the skewers between my thumb and forefinger. A quiet *"ah"* slipped from my mouth as I jerked my hand away and started shaking it in pain. I'd burned myself.

Unable to bear it, I dipped my fingers into the cold water on the table and called out,

"Ice! Urgent! Ice, ice, ice!"

When the ice came, I held a cube between my fingers to cool the burn. Then I took a solid sip of rakı and returned to my real business.

It hurt—but no reason to let it ruin the moment.

By now, the skewers had cooled down a little. The trick was to grip the very tip of the skewer and slide the meat off that way. I actually knew all this—it was just a careless moment. Now I approached the operation more professionally. I took two pieces of lavash, layered them together, gripped the tip of a skewer, and guided the liver pieces between the bread in my left hand, pressing them gently into my palm. I could feel each cube of meat individually through the bread.

Then, without rushing or dragging, I slid the empty skewer off and set it aside at the edge of the table. I carefully laid the little parcel of meat and bread into my plate. On top, I added a generous pinch of onion salad—finely chopped with lots of sumac and red pepper—some ezme, and the freshest tips of the parsley leaves.

The secret was in the final touch: a dash of cumin, a pinch of salt, and plenty of lemon juice.

Once that last step was done, I rolled it tight into a small cone-shaped wrap. It was no longer just a bite of food—it was now a sublime meze. For me, it was two or three bites at most. With every bite, I took a sip of rakı, maintaining a rhythm, a balance of sorts.

After the third mini wrap, I gave up on the double-lavash method. From then on, I used a single layer of bread. But when I went a bit too heavy on the ezme, the delicate lavash would tear under the pressure of the sauce and juices—especially once the rakı began making me careless.

The juices and oils would start to drip down my fingers, trailing toward my forearm. In those moments, I'd quickly drop the wrap onto the plate, gather everything up with a fork, and continue eating piece by piece.

By the time I finished the skewers, I was almost full. But my mouth, my stomach, my mind—my whole body—wasn't satisfied yet. It wanted more. More flavor. More fullness. More of everything, again and again...

45

Satisfaction longed for continuity in pleasure. There was just one last pour left in the bottle. I filled my glass, topped it off with water, and this time I added plenty of ice—even my şalgam had ice now. To cut the salt and soften the rakı, I squeezed a bit of lemon into the şalgam as well.

As I slowly sipped this final glass with some remaining cacık and şalgam, the head waiter returned.
"Going on?" he asked.

I had Adana on my mind—and I thought, *why leave it in my mind when it could be in my stomach?*
"Send in a spicy Adana," I said.
"Right away!" he replied.
"Chef! One spicy Adana!" he called out to the cook.

The cook turned toward me with a smile, as if to say, *keep it coming*. I smiled back—*yes, bring it on.*

The Adana was on its way, but the rakı was nearly gone. You can't have Adana without rakı. It would be a waste of both. I quickly caught the waiter:
"Do you do half bottles?" I asked.
"Bro, I'll bring a full small bottle. Drink what you like—we'll count what's left."
Smart. Fair.

"Great, bring it right away," I said.

Meanwhile, my rakı glass stood empty. The final sip had left behind a cloudy residue at the bottom, stained by the mezze and all I had consumed. I picked up the second glass of the latest pair—the "twin" of the last—and decided it was time for a clean start.

A fresh bottle of rakı arrived, along with another cold water bottle. Everything was chilled. I couldn't resist and dropped a single cube of ice in. There were only a few cubes left in the stainless steel bucket. I simply pointed at it, and the busboy understood—he whisked it away and returned with a full one.

Everything was renewed. I prepared a fresh duble in my clean glass, refreshed the şalgam, and this time squeezed a quarter of a lemon straight into it, dropping the wedge in. I took a sip of rakı, then a mouthful of şalgam.

The meze were nearly gone—quiet now, almost mournful. I didn't mess with them much anymore; the Adana was still coming. The chef was turning the meat on the grill, pressing it with a piece of bread to absorb the fat.
It was necessary, for a good sear. The chef knew that. And so did I.

Once both sides were cooked, he carefully lifted the kebab and transferred it onto a long metal plate. Then he finished the preparation below the counter—it all happened quickly. He pulled the plate out and called:
"Adana, coming up!"

All the tables were full by now. The room buzzed with a constant hum of voices. The chef's voice disappeared into it, but the head waiter could pick it out instantly. He turned toward the grill.

A few other plates were ready too, which he masterfully stacked in his right hand. He came to my table first and placed the Adana in front of me. The plate was covered with triangular lavash, concealing the kebab underneath. It helped keep the food warm—and served as backup bread.

Adana had to be eaten hot. It was fatty, and that meant eating fast.

I removed the lavash slices and placed them aside. The kebab looked plump and perfectly cooked. On the plate were extra onion salad, a grilled tomato split in half, and one grilled green pepper—çarliston.

I was going to wrap it, of course. But the Adana was thick and wide—too big to fit into a single wrap. So I split it down the middle, then again horizontally—four pieces. Four wraps, that was the plan.

The first one I filled with just the meat—to savor the pure taste. It was satisfying.

For the second, I planned something more colorful. I'd use the grilled tomato and pepper. But the tomatoes were too juicy—they needed to be chopped. I peeled them first, removed the seeds, and even then, knowing they'd leak, I used three layers of lavash.

On top, I laid the peeled pepper, halved lengthwise. It was going to be a dense, heavy wrap, so I rolled it carefully, tightly, slowly. As I worked, I refreshed my rakı. Then I took a massive bite of the wrap. I chewed slowly, enjoying every second.

By now, I was fully buzzed—my focus narrowed to taste, nothing else.

At first, there was a mild sting in my mouth. Then came a full-on explosion—a sharp burn like poison, boring into my brain. I struggled to swallow.

I immediately reached for my şalgam—downed it. It wasn't enough. Then water. Then I stuffed the rest of the tomato into my mouth.

"Of! Üf! Püf!"—I gasped aloud. My eyes caught the chef's—he was watching me, chuckling quietly to himself.

That innocent-looking green pepper? A sabotage. I called out to him,
"What the hell, man? Where'd you find this insane heat?"
"Eat it slow, brother—savor it," he said.
"Alright," I answered.

The burn was fierce—but at least it didn't linger too long. It didn't torment you for minutes on end.

I took smaller bites and finished the wrap. Somehow, I'd drained another glass of rakı without realizing it. I topped it up again—but by now, I was really flying. I don't even remember how I ate the rest of the kebab.

I didn't make wraps anymore. I just picked at the remaining meat and salad with my fork. That last glass disappeared with it all.

I was stuffed. Completely, totally full.

I asked for the bill.
"Tea, coffee, dessert?" came a familiar voice, almost whispering.

I couldn't fit another bite in my mouth.
"Just the check," I said.

I paid, and walked out of the grillhouse...

46

As I stepped outside, my senses sharpened by drunkenness, my nose began to pick up every scent around me with strange precision. It was as if distant cigarette smoke and stale beer, the bottled, open-air perfumes used by cheap prostitutes, and the shit-smell sneaking out of bathroom vents—all of it came rushing in from afar. I was aware of every one of them. And for some reason, that awareness brought with it a nameless sorrow.

I could sense all the fine details of life—but I couldn't enter them. I only caught their scent. Inside me was an irresistible curiosity, a primal drive to live—but life itself was pushing me away, giving off only its aroma.

Through the waves of sound, scent, and blurry images, I found myself on İstiklal Avenue. My eyes were on women. The alcohol had surfaced my loneliness, and loneliness, in turn, had awakened a gnawing sexual hunger, laying it bare atop the night.

Hadn't I just slept with Marina the night before?
Clearly, this hunger wasn't physical. Not even physiological.
It was something else—like the way hunger returns every single day.

I was thinking about the night. After evening came the night... and that night, I was definitely going to Babybon. That was certain. I had to find Marina. I had to win her back.

It wasn't just about sex.
I needed to talk to her.
In any language of the world—or even without language at all.
I needed to listen to her pain, and for her to listen to mine.
If needed, we had to understand each other.

Marina was the negative of Ela. Or the positive.
Or maybe neither.

You couldn't really fit people onto a straight line between two absolutes.
They were far too complex for that.
Which is why I began thinking of them side by side.
Ela–Marina. Marina–Ela.
The more I repeated it, the more it condensed into a single name: **ElaMar**.

Yes. I had a lover.
Her name was **ELAMAR**.

47

Before reaching Galatasaray, I wanted to escape—flee from the river that was İstiklal. It wasn't just the urge to get away from the crowd. Everything I'd eaten—all the spicy, sour, salty things, the salads, the alcohol, the remnants of the night before—had created a chemical explosion in my stomach, a kind of digestive diffusion, which had now turned into a sharp pain stabbing up through my tailbone.

So I sped up. As soon as I reached Turnacıbaşı, I turned down and let myself go, hurling downhill toward home.

But the pressure inside me kept building, becoming unbearable. Before long, I couldn't walk anymore. I had to sit down on the edge of the sidewalk and wait for the internal assault to subside.

I was slumped over, a bitter expression frozen on my face. The few passersby who noticed me stared, puzzled—they must've thought I was in some kind of serious pain. And they weren't wrong.

After a while, the pain eased just enough for me to stand and walk again. I barely made it home, each step steeped in agony. I had already begun loosening my belt and unbuttoning my pants as I climbed the stairs.

By the time I entered the apartment, the final and most brutal wave had hit. I almost didn't make it to the toilet—I nearly lost it right there. Locking my legs together, I cried out in pain, shuffling toward the bowl in tiny, desperate steps. Sweat trickled down my spine, my forehead.

With one final push, I got my pants down and landed on the toilet just in time.
And then the release—
a soft, almost erotic groan of relief:
"Offff…"

I stumbled out of the bathroom, wrecked and wrecked again. There was no choice—I had to take a shower. The apartment felt cold, or maybe it was just me. I wrapped myself in whatever towels I could find.

Back in my room, I crawled under the blanket. A faint whistling sound drifted in from the window frames. I pulled over the ragged throw—technically a bedspread, but it always ended up balled at my feet or crumpled on the floor. The fabric was faded, the seams worn and torn in places.

I was trying to warm up.
My feet especially were freezing.

The hot water and the shower had worn me out. The drunkenness had taken on a strange new shape—my head was spinning now, and even my stomach was queasy. But I wouldn't vomit. I had to keep everything inside.

It was still too early for Babybon.
No point in going before noon.

I closed my eyes and tried to sleep.
When I did, it wasn't full darkness.
There were flashes—white lightning strikes flickering across the inside of my eyelids.
I didn't know where they came from or what they meant.

But at least they kept me from thinking.

So I watched them.
Watched the lightning.
My breath became shallow.

That meant I was about to sleep.
First came the sensation of falling—like sliding off the

edge of the bed.
Then I slipped into dark, dense sleep.

48

When I woke up, I couldn't tell the time—but the darkness had deepened, and the city's lights had dimmed. I hadn't moved at all inside the towels. My body felt like a single solid block. I wondered if I'd even be able to get up. For a moment, I thought about giving up on everything—just staying there, sleeping as long as I could, without food, without drink…

But then, I got up to get dressed.

In the mess and the dark of the room, finding clean underwear and socks wasn't easy, but I managed. I went to the bathroom, peed, washed my face. When I came back, my perspective had shifted. The bed no longer looked so inviting. And the loneliness… it had changed too.

Wearing just my underwear, I stepped out onto the balcony. The street in front of Babybon was lively. The movement had a deceptive allure.

I went back inside and looked at the alarm clock on the table.
It was just past 2 a.m.

Perfect timing.

Without overthinking, I started getting dressed. A quick splash of cologne, a comb through the hair—and I was out the door.

49

Having just woken up, I felt like someone who had gotten out of bed in the morning and ended up in a nightclub. I wasn't exactly hungry, but my stomach had tightened. I sat at the bar and ordered a beer.
"Make it a 33," I said.
I didn't really feel like drinking—but you couldn't be in this place sober.

When the beer came, I took the glass, spun the bar stool around, and leaned my back against the counter. I spread my legs wide and placed the glass between them, resting it on the red leather of the stool. I began observing the room as if I weren't really there, like no one could see me. It felt like I was visiting a world designed purely for fantasy.

Strangely, I felt at peace. A constant smile rested on my face.

The women, in their colorful outfits—tight jeans, short skirts, low-cut tops, and tacky dresses—were moving from table to table with that slightly vacant, slightly foolish smile they all wore. The heavy perfume scent that always seemed to evoke sex work was everywhere—floating on the bar's internal currents.

It was a calm but busy night at Babybon. For some reason, there was no live band, but even the piped-in music sounded good. Then, suddenly, the music surged—like a sonic blast—and all the girls poured onto the stage to a pounding dance beat.

This was the moment I had been waiting for.
This scene always made me smile.

The girls moved on stage with nonchalance. They were waiting to be picked, to be taken. That's how they made more money—by being chosen.

My eyes scanned the tables, the girls who hadn't gone up—searching for Marina. But she wasn't there.

Maybe she'd left early for a job?
Those who left early always came back. They waited for a second—or even third—round of work. As long as the club hadn't closed, they always came back. Even if there were only ten minutes left till closing, they'd return, catch the shuttle, and head to the hotel. That was the rule.

So I had to be patient.

I finished my first beer and ordered a large one for the second round. The first had prepared my stomach.

With the second, the bartender dropped a mixed bowl of bar snacks in front of me. The second beer went down easier. The salty snacks helped.

As the drinks flowed, the place became more animated. Girls left and came back. Tables turned over quickly.

I stayed put and kept drinking.
By the third, Marina still hadn't shown up.
At least five girls had come back from jobs. But not her.
Maybe someone had booked her for the whole night.

The fourth beer changed my mood completely.
I stopped obsessing over Marina.
My eyes were now on the other girls.
Maybe I should take one home tonight, I thought.

But something was missing—İsmail Ağa wasn't around.
No sign of the manager either.

Just as I was thinking that, İsmail passed in front of me in his usual rush. Before I could even call his name, he'd disappeared through the side door, heading to the club's backrooms. But five minutes later, he returned.

This time I caught him—gently touching his arm as he passed. He jumped as if I'd hit him with a stick, then turned sharply toward me.

As soon as he saw me, a boyish smile spread across his face.
"Ah, it's you, bro," he said as he came closer. He was smiling—probably thinking about the TV.

As he shook my hand, he bowed his head and body slightly.
He'd taken the TV without pity, but he still showed me respect.
After all, I was a paying customer.

The moment our hands parted, he was about to leave, but I stopped him.
"Wait a second—I need to ask you two things."
He leaned in close, his nose catching a whiff.
"Go ahead, bro," he said.

"I need to get the TV back," I said.
"Bro, I already took that home, rented a car, spent money. It's not coming back."
"Fine," I said. "Then—where's the girl who came that night? Marina—where is she?"

"Marina? Bro, she probably told you that. Her name's Gülbaran. That's what we call her. You mean the limping Romanian girl?"
"Yes, the one who limps—where is she?"

"Bro, she came in really late that night, and the boss fired her. She probably went to work at another place."
"Do you know where she's staying?" I asked.
"She might be at the same place, but you won't find her, bro. Look around—this place is full of girls. Take whoever you want, money's not a problem."
He patted my back.

After the TV thing, he saw me as an old friend.
"No, no," I said sharply. "We'll see."

İsmail Ağa shook my hand again and left.
That handshake meant something. A handshake meant respect.
The manager didn't shake just anyone's hand. That's why

the waiters, the bartenders, the bouncers—they all treated me well.

But the news about Marina being fired…
It wasn't good.
It upset me deeply.

It was probably my fault.
Guilt hit me hard.
And it kept growing.

Now, I had to find her.
Maybe she'd gone over to Bonbon?
İsmail had said the boss fired her—but you could never trust what they said.
To people like them, lies and truths were the same thing.

I asked for the check.
Had they mistreated her?

The bill arrived.
Marina was probably her real name.
They had just slapped Gül on top of it.

I left the money and walked out in quick steps, lost in thought.

50

I really didn't want to go into Bonbon. It was a rip-off, and I knew it. But I couldn't walk past without checking. I had no other leads.

The moment I stepped inside, I saw a line of men in black suits, ties, and hands clasped in front of them. They were slightly bowed at the same angle, standing like mannequins frozen mid-posture—as if trained specifically to hold that position. My entrance stirred them. As I looked around, a bit confused, a bit hesitant, another man in a black suit appeared from the back, shook my hand, and gently touched my left shoulder with his own left hand. He gestured toward the tables closest to the stage and said something like,
"Let's seat you over here, brother."

Those were the most dangerous seats—the ones where the bill gets bloated the most.
"No," I said. "Take me to the back."

He didn't insist. He probably recognized me from Babybon.

As we walked toward the back, the maître d' leaned in close, trying to start a conversation. He was asking pointless questions. His face was narrow, bony. Even though he had shaved meticulously, it looked like the stubble would burst out of his skin at any moment. His cheeks seemed hollowed out from too much shaving.

When we reached the table, I ordered rakı—there was no way a night like this would end with just beer. I didn't keep him waiting. The maître d' walked off in that same slight tilt, confident and swift, his suit hanging on him like a coat on a rack—like there was no body inside.

With the rakı came four or five mezes, standard. No escape from those—they always found their way into the check somehow. But one of them was roasted, warm Antep pistachios—my favorite. The portion was small, barely anything at the bottom of the bowl.

The waiter who brought the tray had already prepared my rakı. I took a sip and settled in.

All the tables in the back were booth-style, lined along the walls. Deep red tones dominated the decor. The walls were clad in rustic, fake stone. In the dim light, it looked nice—but if they ever turned on the fluorescent lights during cleaning, the place would be unrecognizable. At that point, no one would perceive it as it was now.

Everything was in place. I began scanning the girls one by one.
The odds of Marina being here were near zero.
I looked around hopelessly.

These were high-end prostitutes—Russians, Belarusians, Ukrainians—flawless white skin, blond hair, pink cheeks, all parading through the space. Marina was almost as beautiful, but I couldn't picture her limping around this place—and neither could the pimp here.

"I'll just drink my rakı, knock out, and be done with it," I told myself.

I downed half the glass.
Drinking rakı on top of beer shifted my thoughts.

The maître d' who had seated me noticed the change. I was more relaxed now, leaning into my seat, looking around with interest, smiling. He walked toward me with steady, deliberate steps, buttoning his jacket and smiling.

This time, though, he sat right next to me.
At clubs like this, managers sometimes sat at the tables of customers they respected. It was normal.
Of course, in places like this, *respect* came from something else—it depended on how much you could spend, how far you were willing to go.

They knew me from Babybon.
They knew my capacity.
That was the source of respect.

He opened the conversation with:
"Anything you need?"

It was a way to ease into offering a girl.
That's how the *cold cuts season* always began.

I thought about what I wanted—but what could this man with a leathery, weathered face really offer me?
Under the club's dim purple light, his skin looked almost moldy.

He pulled a long Marlboro from his right jacket pocket and offered it to me. I took it. He lit it for me, then lit his own.

The way he inhaled—
it was like his organs weren't flesh but rusted iron pipes.

The smoke first came out of his nose, then, just as he said,
"Brother, if there's a girl you like, I'll call her,"
it drifted naturally from his mouth.

Before the smoke had even fully left him, he took another drag.
For some reason, I felt like asking a rude question.
Alcohol did that to me sometimes.

"Where do these women stay?"

He froze for a second—then chuckled.
"Brother, different places," he said.
"Generally?" I asked.
"Mostly in hotels. All together," he replied.

"So, which one do you like?" he asked again.

I looked around the club—
they all looked the same.
If I picked one, I'd regret not picking another.
And I couldn't afford to take them all.

Just then, a girl in a white dress walked by the stage.
The dress looked like something from a recycled ballet costume—flared skirt, tight ruched top.
She was very young.
She swayed exaggeratedly in her dress.

I gave a subtle nod—head and eyes.
"That one in white," I said.
"Got it, brother," he said, standing up at once.

He put out his cigarette in an ashtray on one of the nearby tables as he walked away.

51

I had assumed the girl was Russian, but she turned out to be Moldovan. She sat quietly, politely. She had already picked up enough Turkish to understand me. They learned quickly. She sat next to me in a demure, ladylike way.

Her face was shaped like a spoon. She had clumsily applied blush to her cheeks.

"Do you know Marina?" I asked.
"No," she said, drawing the word out.

"Marina—the one who limps, Romanian—don't you know her?" I pressed.

"Why are you asking?"

"Just curiosity," I said. "Just curiosity."

"Marina doesn't come here anymore. She's working somewhere else now. I know, but I can't tell you. The boss would get mad."

"Where is she staying?"

"Where everyone else stays."

"And where's that?"

"At a hotel in Dolapdere."

"Do you know the name, the address of the hotel?"

"I can't say... no..."
It was clear she was scared.
I didn't push her any further.

"My drink is finished," she said, giving me a pleading look—hoping I'd order another one for her.
But I didn't.
"All right," I said simply.
I had gotten enough information.

The girl got up with a sour expression.
I asked for the bill.
The skeletal maître d' had written it fairly. I paid and left.

These clubs, these women... they were suffocating me.

I made it home.
I didn't turn on the lights.
I didn't even change my clothes—not even my shoes.
I stood at the balcony, looking down at the street.

The front of the clubs was still bustling. Taxis coming and going. People drifting in and out.

It hurt me to think that someone could just disappear like that.
I couldn't stomach it.

I had a plan forming in my head.
The night wasn't over.
The day wasn't over.

My mind was buzzing, but I didn't feel the drunkenness.
I'd had four or five beers and a small bottle of rakı.

I didn't hate anyone—
but somehow, I was angry.

It was 5 a.m.
I called Hikmet, the taxi driver. Asked him to come around 6.
"I can't promise," he said.
"I'll pay good money," I said.
"All right," he replied.

I went back to the balcony and kept watching the night burn itself out.
When I got tired, I came inside, dragged one of the old dining chairs over to the table, sat parallel to it, and leaned my right elbow on the surface.

I lit a cigarette.

Then I went back out to the balcony.
Morning was starting to show its face now.
Everyone had left the clubs—except the girls.

It was five minutes to six.

I held my cigarette between two fingers, tilted it at an angle, and flicked it off the balcony.

Then I went back inside.

52

The moment I stepped inside, my phone rang. It was Hikmet, the taxi driver. In a low voice, he said,
"Brother, I'm here. I'm downstairs."
"Okay," I said, and hung up.

I grabbed my overcoat and headed out.

Hikmet had pulled the taxi right up to the front of the closed-up kiosk. He was parked so close there was no way he could open his door from the driver's side.
He had trapped himself inside the cab.

I got in and sat beside him. He immediately reached for the ignition.
"Wait. Hold on," I said.
"Turn on the meter and wait."

He turned and looked at me, confused.
"Brother, where are we going?" he asked.
"I said wait, just wait. What's the harm in waiting?"
"Okay," he said.

He offered me a cigarette. I took it, and we both lit up.

He had chosen a good spot—where we could see Sadri Alışık Street from a certain angle, and Babybon's door too. The movement outside had died down.

Before long, a white minibus pulled up across from Babybon. It turned off its headlights and waited.
The driver got out, lit a cigarette, and then went up and knocked on Babybon's door.

A short while later, the door opened.
The girls, carrying their handbags and wearing coats or jackets, started pouring out, laughing, into the minibus.

They looked so cheerful—like schoolkids on a field trip. Unnecessarily happy, considering the life they were living.

Even after everyone had boarded, the minibus didn't move.
It waited.
And so did we.

"Hikmet, give me another cigarette," I said.
He handed one over.

"What are we doing exactly, brother?" he asked as he passed it to me.
"We're going to follow that minibus once it moves," I said.

"The club's service van?" he asked, uneasy.
"Yes," I said.

He looked at me like I'd lost my mind.

But my eyes stayed on the minibus.

Then one of the black-suited men came out of the club—tie undone, shirt open almost down to his belly.
He got into the front passenger seat.
As soon as he was inside, the minibus headlights blinked on.

Hikmet reached for the ignition again.
"Wait," I said.
"Let them turn onto Turnacıbaşı first. Then we move."

"Brother, you've turned into a real detective," Hikmet said, laughing nervously.

The minibus pulled away, heading down Turnacıbaşı toward Galatasaray.
We followed behind, keeping a good distance.

It was the brightest, emptiest, coldest hour of the city.
It made you wonder if time itself could turn back from here.

It didn't.
But soon the light would stand up,
the ground would evaporate,
and people would flood back into the streets.

As we crossed İstiklal, the taxi slowed down.
There were still a few pedestrians lingering on the avenue—

they never seemed to end.
Always moving.

Then we passed near the fish market, crossed the
boulevard, and disappeared into the deeper parts of the city.

I no longer knew where we were.
I still didn't really know Istanbul.

"We're heading toward Dolapdere, right?" I asked Hikmet.
He nodded silently.

He was thoughtful, clearly not thrilled about what we were doing—
but he was already in it now.

53
The minibus stopped somewhere.
It wasn't exactly a street, nor a proper avenue.
Maybe in daytime traffic, it would have a name—
but right now, it was nameless.

A neighborhood that had shed whatever aesthetic it once had—
everything rough, patched-up, broken.

The building where the minibus stopped was technically a hotel,
but it didn't look like one.

Six stories, stretched out long along the street,
its windows sunken in like purple bruised eyes.

The entrance was tucked into a corner.
Without the battered "Hotel" sign above the door, no one would have guessed it was a hotel.
But it didn't look like an apartment building or an office either.
Just a flat plane of windowed eyes…

The building's color was the raw color of plaster—
almost no color at all.

When the minibus stopped, we kept driving, made a U-turn a bit farther up, and parked about 50 meters away, on the right.

Nobody had gotten out of the minibus yet.
Then, the suited man sitting in the front hopped out, opened the side door—
and the women began to spill out, laughing, swinging their handbags just like before.
Same careless cheer, same mechanical gestures.

Once everyone was out, the suited man went inside the building for a moment,
then immediately came back out, got into the minibus, and it pulled away—
melting into the color of the night.

Hikmet, the taxi driver, watched all this unfold beside me with the same bewilderment.

Then he turned and looked at me.
"Brother, what exactly are you doing?" he asked.

I didn't answer.
I handed him the fare.
"You can go," I said.

Hikmet gave me my change, then sped off.

Once the taxi disappeared, I edged closer to the hotel—
but I still didn't know exactly what I was going to do.
Why was I really here?

I slipped into the entrance of a neighboring building where
I could watch the hotel door.
It sheltered me from the cold and kept my surveillance
hidden.

Ten minutes later, another minibus arrived.
It stopped in the same spot.
Same routine—
the suited man got out first, opened the door,
and the women started getting out, counted one by one as
they did.

They were checked in, handed over to someone inside, I
guessed.

I watched the women carefully.
There was no way I could miss Marina.
There weren't many limping women among the club
workers.

More women were pouring out of this minibus—
they seemed endless.

My hands were starting to shake from the cold.
I lit a cigarette.

I bent my neck forward instinctively, the way a hunter
leans toward prey.
I adjusted my line of sight with each figure that appeared.

And finally—
I saw her.

She was wearing a red jacket over tight jeans.
Limping as always.
Moving toward the hotel door with a sadness clinging to
her body.

I held my breath.
I had spotted my target.
I was completely serious now.

I waited another half-hour by the entrance.
By then, morning had broken.
The streets had started filling up.

Finally, I stepped out from my hiding place and walked
toward the hotel.

54
The reception desk was tucked away immediately to the
left of the entrance, almost hidden under the staircase.
It was far smaller than you'd expect for such a massive
building.

The lobby was built with the same minimalist mindset.
There was just a single sitting group—enough for four
people—positioned right in front of the elevator hall.

In fact, the lobby and the elevator hall were essentially the
same space.

There was no one around—
neither at the reception desk,
nor in the lobby.

The only light came from the glass panels of the entrance
door.
But even that was muted—
the glass was darkened with age and grime.

A crystal chandelier hung above the sitting area, its missing
bulbs exposing gaps like missing teeth.
The place was dim—almost bordering on dark.

I quietly walked up to the elevator.
The air was heavy, thick with the scent of decay.
Everything smelled old.

When I pressed the elevator call button, a sharp "crack"
sound echoed.

It startled me—lifting me slightly off the ground.
I looked around—still no one.

When the elevator finally arrived, it made a similar sharp noise.
I grabbed the door handle and pulled.
Then a folding panel slid open like an old accordion.

The elevator cabin was lined with fake wood paneling—
formica—
the seams peeling up, swollen with time.

There were six floors.
My hand went instinctively to the 3rd.
I pressed it.

55
A long corridor greeted me.
The elevator opened at one end of it.

Doors lined the right-hand side of the hallway,
but on the left, there were secondary corridors branching off.
It wasn't a common layout for a hotel—
especially not one in the city center.

I started walking down the main corridor.
At the start of each secondary corridor, there was a gate—
iron bars like a prison door.

Because they were set back from the main hall, you couldn't see them from one end—

but as you walked, you'd find one at every branching corridor.
Each was locked with a big, heavy padlock.

At the entrance of one of the side corridors, I paused and watched.
Girls were moving between rooms, half-naked,
wearing just their underwear,
laughing.

They were trapped here somehow—
but they didn't look imprisoned.
Not in the way they moved.

I lingered briefly at the entrance of each side corridor.
The floor was covered in a low, worn-out, dirty carpet.
The baseboards had come loose everywhere,
but none had fallen off.

The rooms on the opposite side faced the street.
There was no sound from them.
It felt like no one lived there at all.

When I reached the end of the corridor,
I noticed that one room's door was open.
I heard the sound of a vacuum cleaner inside.

I pushed the door open slightly and peered in.
An old woman was cleaning the room.

So—someone must actually stay here after all.

The vacuum cleaner stopped.
The woman noticed me.
She approached the door.
I wanted to turn and run—
but I was frozen in place.

She smiled warmly at me.
"Did you lose your room?" she asked.

"Yes... I must've come to the wrong floor," I said.

She nodded.
"Yes, your room is on the 5th floor. Room 508," she said, then went back to her cleaning.

Had she been trying to give me a signal?
Or was it a trap?

I wasn't sure.

As the girls' laughter echoed behind me, I made my way back down the long corridor and returned to the elevator.

The elevator was still on the same floor.
I stepped in and pressed 5.

The 5th floor was built exactly the same way—
but newer.
Renovated.

Even the smell was different—
cleaner.

But the iron gates at the head of each corridor were still there.
Only now they were decorative—
made of ornamental black wrought iron.

Everything on this floor was dominated by a deep maroon color.
The carpets, the cherrywood doors, the beige wallpaper patterned with maroon designs—
nothing but beige and maroon everywhere.

Room 508 was almost exactly in the center of the main corridor,
and directly across from it was one of the secondary corridors.

This floor was quieter than the third.
No half-naked women running from room to room.
There were still sounds coming from behind some doors, but it was different here—
calmer.

Pinned to the door of 508 was a white envelope.

When I instinctively reached for the door handle,
the door swung open.
The envelope dropped to the floor.

On it was written:
"Dear [Name], welcome to Dolapdere Hotel. – Management."

My name was on the envelope.

I picked it up and stepped inside.
The room had been prepared for me somehow.

It was just like the corridor—newly renovated.
Simple, tasteful, and freshly cleaned.

I sat on the bed, still holding the envelope.
I opened it.
Inside was a folded sheet of paper—a letter:

"I knew you would come here.
The room was reserved for you.
It's already paid for.
I will reach out to you.
– Marina."

I was stunned.
And a little frightened too.

There was a security latch on the door.
I slid it shut.
After all, this room was mine now.

I started undressing to take a shower.
The bathroom was comfortable—
much more so than the one in my apartment.

The water heated quickly, and the temperature mixed well.
The towels were pure white and soft.

I wrapped myself in as many as I could find—
one around my body,
another around my head like a turban—
and returned to the room.

I grabbed a beer from the minibar,
lay down on the bed,
and started sipping.

I was exhausted.
Sleep was creeping in.

I drank the beer quickly—
I was thirsty—
and soon, I drifted off into sleep.

56
I was in a deep sleep when a knock at the door woke me.
At first, I couldn't remember where I was.
Then I gathered the towels wrapped around me and went to the door.

Through the peephole, I saw the old cleaning lady from the third floor.

Without unlocking the security latch, I opened the door slightly.
"Yes?" I said.

The woman was holding a set of keys.
"You dropped your room key on the third floor," she said.
"I brought it back."

I took the key and went back inside.
Got dressed.
Returned the towels to the bathroom.

I sat on the edge of the bed for a while,
thinking about leaving,
running away—
when suddenly the room phone rang.

I picked it up.
It was Marina's voice.

"The key you just received opens the iron gate across the corridor from your room. Open it with the key, then go back to your room and wait," she said.
And she hung up.

I got up to follow her instructions.
I unlocked the security latch—
then wedged the door open with something, so it wouldn't lock behind me.

I crossed to the iron gate across the hall.
There was no padlock—
just a door lock, like the room doors had.

The key the cleaning lady had brought fit perfectly.
I unlocked it.
Left the iron gate slightly ajar—
and went back to my room.
I lay down and waited.

Not even ten minutes passed when there was a knock at my door.

I opened it.
It was Marina.

But she was different this time—
not the same as the girl who had come to me before.

She was wearing a sheer, gauzy nightgown.
Underneath, her red lingerie was clearly visible.
Her hair was styled, her makeup fresh.

She slipped inside with a soft push against me, smiling.

"Lie down on the bed," she said.

I didn't resist.
I lay down.

She sat beside me and placed one of my hands on her chest.

"I knew you would come," she said.
"You're brave enough to come."

I opened my mouth to speak—
but she pressed her fingers gently against my lips,
silencing me.
Then she leaned down and gave me a soft, wet, deep kiss.

Without hesitation, she started unbuttoning my shirt.
Her hands felt bigger now, stronger—

I felt small in them.
Every move was confident, decisive.

Within minutes, she had undressed me.
She had all the initiative—
I had surrendered completely.

Then she lay down beside me.
There was no need for her to undress—
everything she wore seemed to dissolve at a touch.

She allowed me only as much as I desired—
no more, no less.

I stayed there, with Marina, all through the day until nightfall.
And during that long day,
Marina told me the secret behind everything that had happened—
and everything that was about to happen.

57
In the evening, I was quiet at home.
I couldn't quite figure out where anyone stood anymore in the landscape of my life.

I had never thought Marina was the kind of person she turned out to be.
Pity and compassion had drawn me to her—
but what I found was someone completely different.

Now, I felt far away from everything.

Tomorrow was Sunday, my last free day.
On Monday, work would start again.
I'd be buried in the problems of the construction site,
the workers, the consulate...

And Ela—
she was still, technically, my girlfriend.
But she was gone.
Vanished.
It was as if she had loosened the strings holding me up,
allowed me to live through all of this.

I felt guilty toward her—
and strangely, the guilt tied me even closer to her.

Every man who cheats probably feels this,
maybe cheating itself was a form of trying to renew, to
cleanse oneself.

I made a decision:
no more drinking until Monday.

My head had ached enough,
my stomach burned enough,
my pockets emptied enough.

I could eat at home—
I had to save some money.

All I really needed was water.
My body was desperate for rest.

I brought a few liter-bottles of water to the bed,
lay down,
and drank whenever my mouth went dry.
Every now and then, I got up for the bathroom.

I slept for hours—
slept and slept...

I must have stayed in bed for 14, maybe 15 hours.

When I woke up,
I wasn't hungry—
but I felt dried out.

I kept drinking water.
My head didn't ache anymore;
instead, it felt completely empty,
as if air had been pumped into my veins and brain.

I didn't want to get up from bed.

My body had rested—
but the wild animal inside me had awakened.

I was unbearably aroused.
Even after going to the bathroom, it didn't subside.

Just yesterday, I had spent hours with Marina—
yet my body had already regenerated itself,
as if memory and logic had nothing to do with it.

I didn't want to touch myself,
but the tension built up inside me—
a heavy, swelling pressure in my abdomen,
like a false pregnancy.

My mind floated to the idea of buying a few beers, drinking
until I passed out.

The creature that housed me was never satisfied—
never done eating, drinking, wanting.
Meanwhile, my mind, my heart, my soul lived in another
world entirely—
a nobler, cleaner world.

Maybe that was the root of my self-destructive urges,
this unbearable split inside me.

I wasn't hungry.
I was thinner.
My stomach was flat.

I lit a cigarette and went to the bathroom.
It was easier to be there, sitting, letting the smoke fill my
hollow body.
My head spun lightly.

I grabbed a book on my way in—
I couldn't stay in the bathroom without something to read.
Mostly, I read beginnings—
introductions, back covers—
rarely could I dive into the middle of things.

When the cigarette burned out, I stayed sitting for a while longer,
then finally stood up.
My legs tingled from sitting too long.

I lay back down in bed.

"Sleeping is the best thing," I said, glancing down at my restless body.

Right at that moment—
someone knocked on the door.

I wasn't expecting anyone.
I flinched.
Pulled myself together,
straightened my clothes,
and went to the door.

In one swift move, I opened it.

Standing there was the same Gypsy beauty I had seen before—
the same upright posture,
the same graceful balance on the balls of her feet.

She had tied a scarf loosely around her head,
more like an accessory perched there than a covering.

The light from the stairwell behind her silhouetted her body,
and the lines of her legs showed faintly through her skirt.

She stood smiling at me—
her large, slightly crooked teeth visible in the dim light.

I froze, staring.
And she stared back.

For a brief second, her eyes dropped,
noticing the awkward bulge beneath my loose pajamas.
She quickly looked away.

All of this happened in the span of a few heartbeats.

Then she spoke:
"Brother, do you have any old clothes?
We're trading old things for new laundry baskets and tubs."

I tried to picture what exactly she was proposing,
but I couldn't.

"Yeah, yeah," I said. "This whole place is full of old stuff.
Wait here—I'll gather some things."

I turned back inside, rummaging half-heartedly through old clothes.
I wasn't really trying to find anything—
just stalling, thinking.

I passed through the hallway into the kitchen,
then into the living room,
repeating the motions,
pretending to search.

When I passed by the hallway again, I said:
"Come inside a little, it's freezing.
There's a lot to sort through."

She hesitated—
then stepped inside just a little,
leaving the door half-closed.

Hand on her hip, she said,
"Brother, be quick, the others are waiting."

I watched her out of the corner of my eye—
the perfect upright curve of her figure.
My heart pounded.

For a moment, I fought a dangerous impulse—
but pulled myself back.
The risk, the possibility of disaster—
getting into trouble with her whole clan—
it loomed large in my mind.

And yet, the wild part of me strained at the leash.

I decided to be careful.

I grabbed a bag of old clothes I had found and handed it to her.
She smiled, took it.

As she turned to leave, I gently touched her arm—
nothing forceful, just a brief, human contact.

She paused.
Looked back at me.

There was a flicker of something between us—
curiosity, confusion, a question neither of us fully
understood.
But no violence, no pressure.

"Thank you, brother," she said quietly.
And she slipped out the door, disappearing down the
hallway.

I stood there, heart still racing—
but at peace with myself.

58
The Gypsy girl had shaken me.
Marina had shaken me.
And Ela—
with her absence—
was constantly shaking me.

I went into the shower.
Stayed there a long time, unable to come out.

Thoughts about the Gypsies and the wild stories told about
making love to them swirled in my head.
How long would I be considered impure now?
Forty days?
Two months?
Four?

I didn't care.
By their standards, I had always been impure anyway.

Toward evening, I went out to buy some beer.

Work at the construction site wasn't going well.
They were satisfied with me—
but things weren't going well.

Maybe it was my inexperience, my greenness.
Something was always slipping through the cracks.

The workers were sly—
village-smart.
They liked me, or pretended to,
but everything revolved around their own interests.

It was all a game of survival,
a game of money.
How much they earned,
how much they could slack off without getting caught—
that's all they cared about.

I was running nonstop,
wearing myself down,
but still, I didn't give up.

The hangovers,
the women,

were exhausting me more than necessary—
but I pushed on.

Sometimes,
I wouldn't sleep at all—
just show up at the site,
the scent of alcohol like gunpowder on my breath,
still running around.

Sweat would drip from my lower back,
the soles of my feet would blister—
and still, I ran.

The contractor company had bought a Skoda pickup truck—
for supply runs and errands—
but there was no driver.
So I drove it.

On top of everything else,
I started doing outside errands too.

Learning Istanbul behind the wheel made it easier.
I often went down to Perşembe Pazarı.
We had made deals with a few suppliers there.

I would go, pick things out, and buy them—
slowly learning the materials we used.

Usually, the requests came from the site foremen and team leaders.
I tried to understand what they wanted,

took notes,
then went down to the market to find it.

Sometimes I got it right.
Sometimes wrong.
Sometimes I misunderstood completely.

The best part about the Skoda was that most of the time,
I got to keep it with me.

It was useful,
even if I had to take one or two guys along sometimes.
At least my feet were off the ground.

Only when the contractor's main site manager showed up
without his own car did they ask for it back.
Otherwise—
the Skoda was mine.

59

That winter was relentless with rain.
The rain constantly disrupted our work.

That year, I learned to hate the rain—
and that hatred stayed with me for years afterward.

A site worker never loved the rain.

The most difficult tasks for me were the outdoor jobs—
especially anything involving concrete.

I didn't really know the work well.
The foremen and workers must have seen that.
I had become a plaything in their hands.

I was struggling with something that should have been easy.
Maybe everyone, even unconsciously, wanted the work to fail.

And it did.

During a concrete pour, a formwork collapsed.
The entire street flooded with wet concrete.
We spent the whole night washing the streets down.

The incident crushed me.
I was too sensitive.

I went to the bathroom, put my head in my hands—
and cried.

It was the first time I had cried in a long, long while.

The Americans, despite everything, didn't push too hard to have me replaced.
They showed surprising patience.

The second disaster happened inside the building.

We were pouring columns and beams to reinforce a historic structure.
During the pour, the concrete suddenly disappeared through

a hole in the ground.
Later, we discovered there was a hidden underground tunnel—
and we had unknowingly filled it with fifteen cubic meters of concrete.

Maybe these were ordinary mishaps on construction sites.
But my nerves were worn thin.

Through all this, Ela was still by my side.

We didn't appear together much on-site.
We didn't want anyone to guess we were involved.

But she was there.
She had returned after the holiday break—
as if nothing had happened.

We resumed our normal life:
going out in the evenings,
eating at meyhanes,
then either heading to her place on the other side of town,
or me wandering the city alone,
or going home to sleep.

On nights when Ela went back to her place,
I had started meeting up with Deniz.

Sometimes at Urban,
sometimes under the Atlas cinema,
sometimes at the bars tucked away in Nevizade.

We were seriously talking about finding an apartment together.

Winter had taken a firm hold.
Conditions at Ahmet's apartment were wearing me down.

Ela wasn't happy either.
She was always cold there,
never wanted to stay long.

From a bohemian point of view, the apartment was perfect—
antique furniture, great location, endless character.

But reality was harder.

It just wasn't working anymore.

60
It was another Saturday when Ela and I met up,
and we were restless.
Bored.

I was rummaging through the little knick-knacks on top of the console—
small boxes, figurines, bits of forgotten objects.

I picked up a small box shaped like a chest.
When I opened it,
inside was something wrapped in cigarette cellophane,
then again wrapped in the thin foil inside a cigarette pack.

I unwrapped it—
a dried, greenish nugget of marijuana.

"Ela! Look what I found!" I called out.

She rushed over, smiling.
"What are we going to do?" she said.

"We're going to roll it and smoke it—what else?" I said.

There was no rolling paper in the house,
so I ran downstairs to the corner shop.
I bought some papers and a pack of Maltepe cigarettes.

Maltepe was good for this—
a slow burn, the right tradition.

Clumsily, I rolled a joint,
using one of my business cards as a makeshift filter.

We sat cross-legged on the floor mattress in the little side room,
and smoked it.
When we finished the first one,
I quickly rolled a second.

Before lighting it,
I dashed back downstairs to buy some beer—
our mouths were desert dry.

We smoked the second one slowly,
sipping beer in between.

Soon, we were both feeling lightheaded—
pleasantly dizzy.

Ela wasn't traditionally "sexy"—
but there was a hidden beauty in her,
something quiet, something smoldering.

She took off her jeans,
still wearing her shirt,
and began moving lazily around the room,
swaying,
giving me sly, smoky looks.

It was a side of her I wasn't used to—
a playful, slightly wicked mood.

She was tipsy, relaxed,
her movements unselfconscious.

Her legs were slender, almost delicate—
even when she pressed her knees together,
there was still a slight gap between her thighs.

It made her seem both innocent and somehow incredibly
sensual.

From where I lay,
I asked her to step closer to the window—
to stand in the soft light,
her legs together.

I just watched her like that,
silent, breathing in the sight of her.

Even so,
she remained shy—
not eager to reveal too much of herself.

I asked softly,
"Would you take off your underwear?"

She hesitated,
blushing slightly—
but she did.

Her body was natural, untouched—
the hair above her pubis thick, dark,
like something out of a 70s film.

I asked her to turn around.
She turned.

I asked her to bend slightly—
and she did,
only a little.
Tentative.

"More," I said, gently but firmly.

She looked back at me, embarrassed.
"I'm shy," she whispered.

"Come here, then," I said, smiling.

Without losing her modesty,
she walked slowly over to me,
lay down beside me on the floor mattress.

We kissed for a long time,
slow, wet, deep kisses.

Then I carefully guided her to turn over,
face-down.
And we moved together naturally,
gently,
finding each other in a new way.

Ela's body always had a strange mystery to it.
She was tight—
but never quite yielding.
She would let you in,
but you never felt fully enveloped, fully accepted.

Even after climax,
something still felt missing,
an emptiness you couldn't explain—
which only made you want her more.

Maybe that strange distance,
that incomplete satisfaction,
was what sometimes drove me away from her—
toward Marina,
toward Afet,
toward Deniz…

61
Deniz and I met up again at Urban.

Urban was full, as always,
of half-intellectual, self-important types.

That day, Ahmet had come too.
We walked out together afterward.

Whenever Ahmet showed up, Ela usually headed home.
Ahmet knew about us,
but there was still a sense of awkwardness—
Ela was like family to him.

At Urban, Deniz had started flirting shamelessly with Ahmet—
locking eyes with him,
laughing madly,
pressing her large breasts against him every chance she got,
constantly fidgeting and adjusting herself for effect.

It was obvious where this was headed.
She was going to end up with Ahmet without ever having anything happen between her and me.

So be it.
We could stay friends.
We were going to be housemates anyway.
And Ela was in the picture.

Becoming live-in lovers was complicated—
it strained everything.

Besides, Deniz wasn't particularly beautiful—
big-chested, thin-legged, short, freckled.
Nothing like Ela, Marina, or even the Gypsy girl.

But bodily desire was different—
it didn't care about comparison.
It wanted variety.
New experiences.

Still, I had pushed the thought of Deniz out of my mind.

Ahmet, for his part, kept his distance—
but he wasn't immune to the attention either.
He chuckled to himself,
his face giving little away,
but it was clear he was enjoying it.

We got hungry after a while.
When we left Urban, we wandered over to Nevizade.
Collapsed into a meyhane.

Deniz's laughter was endless,
rolling over everything.

I focused on eating,
sipping my rakı,
watching people come and go.

At that moment,
I didn't want to sleep with anyone.
I was just disgusted with myself.

When we left,
Deniz tried to insist on continuing the night,
but neither Ahmet nor I had the energy for it.
Not after working all day on the construction site.

It was almost midnight.
Deniz went home.
Ahmet and I stumbled back to the apartment.

The next day,
Deniz woke me up with a phone call.

She said she had found an apartment in Cihangir.
Her voice was trembling with excitement.

"Come by in the afternoon—let's take a look," she said.

We set a time around three.
I called before heading out to get the address.

The apartment was in a good spot—
right on the main street.

It was a ground-floor unit.
Not bad.

It had been renovated,
but it still clung to the smell of the old building underneath.

"I like it," I said quietly to Deniz.
She smiled and said, "Me too,"
trying not to let the realtor overhear.

Then we switched tactics.
Started trashing the place.

"This place won't do," we said.
"It's falling apart."
"It's a ground floor."
"Opens onto a back garden."
"No security."

On and on we went—
until it was almost like we were begging for a discount.

As soon as we fell silent,
the agent pounced—
asking questions about our jobs,
how we'd pay,
how they could trust us.

Eventually, he dropped the price to the lowest he could authorize.

It wasn't bad.
We would split it between the two of us.

"We'll think about it," we said, and walked out.

Once outside,
I said to Deniz, "I think it's good."

She agreed—
she liked it too.

I left her some money for the deposit
and hurried back to work.

62
Within a few days,
we had moved in.

Deniz's belongings were enough to furnish the place.
As for me,
I just brought over a mattress for my room—
with Ahmet's permission,
I grabbed it from the crumbling old apartment.
No cost.

The new apartment itself was decent in shape.
I took the back room—
the one with windows facing a small backyard.

It was, plainly, a garden-level flat.

There was even a built-in closet,
enough to stash most of my things.
The rest I kept packed in a suitcase—
a setup perfectly suited to my nomadic life.

Ela and I had begun sleeping together more comfortably in
this house, in this room.
Sometimes, I still went back to the old place—
I still had the keys.

But honestly, that old apartment was freezing—
worse than sleeping outside.

Even though the Cihangir place was warmer,
I couldn't bring myself to like it.

Something about it unsettled me.
Maybe it was Deniz's behavior—
maybe just the tension of living with a woman.

I didn't know what time would bring,
but one thing was certain:
I wasn't going to stay long.

Deniz and I had already started clashing over lifestyle.
She wanted a life with a sense of refinement—
tablecloths, matching cutlery, neatly arranged plates.

I wanted to throw down a newspaper on the table,
slice some cheese,
rip some bread,
drizzle some honey,
and just eat.

And that's exactly what I did.

We had begun to irritate each other.
I craved simplicity.
She craved appearances.

She had moved into this apartment dreaming of a more stylish, curated life.
I had moved because it was simply warmer.

Ahmet had started visiting more often whenever he was in Istanbul.
It was obvious why:
Deniz's interest in him,
and his growing interest in her.

One day,
I caught them.
But I didn't say anything.

That day,
we were all at home together.
Later, Ahmet and I left to head to the construction site.

But midway,
Ahmet suddenly said,
"Something came up,"
hailed a cab,
and took off.

A few minutes later,
I got in a taxi too—
but instead of going to work,
I went back to the house.

As I turned onto our street,
I saw Ahmet slip into the building.
I followed quietly behind.

By the time I opened the door,
they were already in the living room,
half-undressed, tangled together.

Without letting them see me,
I pulled the door shut again,
caught a cab—
and this time,
actually went to the construction site.

63
Delays at the construction site had triggered changes.
Small but important interventions—
the contractor company's boss had appointed his uncle as
our new project manager.

The man was an old Shell executive and a master Freemason—
short, goat-bearded, sharp-eyed.

We got along well enough.
He had started backing me,
but he didn't inspire much trust.

Meanwhile, the site manager they had promised from
Russia had finished his previous job
and was sent over to support me.

Now there were two chiefs.
Two heads.

The mood was souring.
Ahmet wasn't himself.
Ela wasn't either.

We all just wanted to finish the job and get out—
or find something else altogether.

Ahmet had some plans brewing in his head,
but he wasn't saying much yet.

I wanted to leave too,
but I had no idea what I would do afterward.

Everyone was stuck in a kind of void.
No one could get out.

We were just flailing.

From the site to the apartment—
sometimes alone,
sometimes with Ela.

If Ahmet was around,
from the site to a bottle of rakı—
sometimes with Ela,
sometimes without her.

Endless troubles on-site.
Constant runs to Perşembe Pazarı in the Skoda—
buying, fetching, hauling.

Why was I doing this?
I didn't even know anymore.

Was I the purchasing agent?
The architect?
The site manager?

What was I?

Fridays were filled with meetings with the Americans.
There were too many bosses.

Our own company's bosses.
The Turkish contractor chiefs and managers.
The American contractor chiefs and managers.
The consulate's control officers and their supervisors.
Security personnel.
Safety officers.
Other engineers.
Electricians.
Mechanical engineers.

They never ended.

I was exhausted.
Suffocating.

I needed to run.
I had to escape.

64
Hatred.

We were filled with hatred.
Hatred for ourselves,
for our surroundings,
for everything,
for the very conditions that had made us who we were.

And yet,
we kept telling ourselves,
"We're fine."

- "Yes, yes. We're fine, right Ela?"
- "Yes, we're fine.
  We have jobs, we have salaries, we have insurance.
  We have our meyhanes after work,
  our movie theaters,
  our bookstores,
  our books,
  the joints we roll now and then,
  our bars,
  our nights out,
  money to buy clothes.
  Yes, we're fine.
  We can even save a little money and take a vacation."

- "Yeah, to Bodrum, Datça, Çeşme…"
- "We'll go.
  Of course we'll go.
  We're fine…"

But hatred?
We were full of it.

More than anything,
I hated the workers.

I couldn't understand how anyone had ever believed
that workers could be revolutionary.

They were miserable,
steeped in wretchedness—
and their misery wasn't because of their material
conditions,
not really.

It came from themselves.
Even beggars, I thought,
had more dignity,
more honesty.

And the Gypsies—
they were gods compared to them.
Afet—
Afet was a Gypsy goddess.

The workers—
their minds were enslaved.
Their pensions, their insurance,
their illusions of an endless existence—
it was all a lie.

No matter what they did,
they would never reach better days,
never touch the light.

A hopeless longing,
a futile struggle...

They had created so many things to lose—
they had chained themselves to fear,
to a fear that only grew larger as they grew older.

They were far from any real revolution.
They had changed.
They had adapted.
They had lost hope.

And we hated our work.
Our jobs.
Being salaried.

It was killing us.

65
Monotony...

Everything was flattening out.
Even our sex.

I wasn't feeling pleasure anymore—
I was just doing it for the sake of physical release.

So we said, "Let's get married,"
Ela and I.

Yes,
if everything was this monotonous,
then we might as well marry.

"We're in love," we told ourselves.

Technically, we were.
In tension, too.

We had problems, questions, complexes
that even we didn't fully understand.

So, let's get married.
Get married and keep drinking.
That was the plan.

Drinking was the one thing we excelled at.
An alcoholic marriage—
perfect conditions.

What about our problems?
Not important.
We'd overcome them. Somehow.

I just wanted to see what magic, what secret power there
might be in marriage.

Marriage would trample over us,
erase us—

we knew it—
but we still wanted it.

The same way you long for suicide sometimes.
The same hunger.

Winter...

Winter was reluctantly abandoning Istanbul.

It was washing over Beyoğlu
like a giant penis in the throes of release—
wild, shameless,
and then,
finally,
dying away.

We were exhausted.
Winter had exhausted us.

66
Spring...

How short the brooding season of summer is in Istanbul—
barely a single sitting.
And now it had come.

İstiklal Avenue had multiplied and multiplied...
What to do?

The site manager sent from Russia—Haluk—
hadn't been able to hold on.
He didn't speak the language,
he had joined the project late,
he couldn't adapt.

And so he left—
back to Russia.

Honestly,
our minds had never aligned anyway.
Day and night he blasted Tarkan songs—
the idiot.

After he left,
the old crumbling house was empty again.

When I got out for lunch breaks,
I started going there—
just sitting,
writing a little.

I missed it.

Cihangir felt too cold,
too full of itself.

Deniz's obsession with luxury,
her inflated self-importance,
her sleeping with Ahmet and whoever else—
it was driving me crazy.

I bought a cigar from the kiosk at the entrance to Çiçek
Pasajı and smoked it there.
I really had missed that old house.
That was where I was truly myself.

I needed to get away from the Cihangir apartment,
away from Deniz—
but she had trusted me enough to leave her friends behind
and move in.

I couldn't understand why.

If we had been sleeping together,
it would have made some kind of sense.
But we hadn't.

Before moving in,
we had thought we agreed on everything—
but once we lived together,
it was clear:
we were two completely opposite kinds of people.

That day,
I returned to the site a little late.
I had smoked my cigar and downed two beers in the old
house—
gotten just slightly buzzed.

The construction site had become unbearable.
My hatred was growing.
The Americans, the managers, the chiefs—
I couldn't stand any of them anymore.

I stormed around the site,
acting tough with everyone.
I wanted to lash out at the workers, too—
they were no better than the Americans.
A bunch of morons.

I shouted and cursed at everyone.
Everything they did was wrong.
Everything we were doing was wrong.
The whole job was a disaster.

Inside and out,
I was bursting with curses:
"Fuck them all, fuck them all."

I stormed back to the office.

Even with Ela,
I was being rough.
Her eyes welled up with tears.

"Why?" she asked.
"What's wrong?"

"I'm gonna get the fuck out of here," I said.
"I can't take this anymore, you know?"

She answered calmly,
still chasing real solutions:
"Then let's quit.
Let's talk to Ahmet."

But there was no such solution.
We had no way out.
No one saw it.

We were drowning.
And the more we thrashed,
the bigger our pit of hell became.

While I was still grumbling and cursing to myself,
the mechanical foreman walked in.

"Brother, we need this and that,"
he said, listing off a bunch of parts—
sizes, types, things I'd never even heard of.

I threw an A4 paper down in front of him:
"Write it down!
What do you think I am—
a computer?"

He scrawled out the list in crooked handwriting.
"I'll send someone to pick it up tomorrow," I said.

"Alright, brother," he said, and left.

I held on a little longer.
Then I turned to Ela and said,
"I'm really sick.
I'm going to rest."

I went to the contractor's project manager:
"Sir, I'm very sick.
I'm heading out early."

"Alright, alright," he said.
I must have looked convincingly miserable.

I slipped out of the consulate building—
free for the day.

67

I wandered through the Fish Market.
Spring fruits were out;
I bought a handful of green plums.

I stopped at the kiosk near Çiçek Pasajı,
picked up rolling tobacco, papers, and two cigars.

I walked down İstiklal Avenue
as if walking with an old friend,
as if sneaking off with an old lover.

Sadri Alışık Street was shaded and empty.
I clung to it too as I walked.

I bought some beers from the corner store under the house
and went upstairs.
I spread everything out on the coffee table.
Popped open a beer, tossed the others into the fridge.
Rolled a cigarette from the tobacco I'd just bought.

Turned on the music—
the old house had a good sound system.

I washed the plums, sprinkled them with salt.
They went well with the beer.
Mixed with the flavor of tobacco,
it was a strange, almost alluring taste.

I was content.
I had forgotten the endless problems at the construction site,
the ones that had been pulling me down like a stone.
That was the beauty of leaving—
the problems stayed behind.

I needed to make a plan for the evening.
Today, I had to get away from Deniz and that cursed apartment.

After finishing the first beer,
I grabbed the second, lit one of the cigars.

Drinking—
yes, drinking would give me a way out.

By the time the beers were finished,
night had fallen.

The bowl on the table, which doubled as an ashtray,
was now overflowing with plum pits, cigarette butts, and cigar ashes.

When darkness finally settled,
I felt a calm filling me.
Knowing that work at the site was over for the day made me feel even lighter.
I no longer felt guilty for skipping out.

Then the phone rang.
It was Ela.

"What are you doing?" she asked.

"I'm at Ahmet's place, drinking."

"Why there?"

"I love this place.
Come over."

"Okay, I'm coming."

"Bring beers when you come.
Don't bring just a few—
bring as many as you can carry!"

We laughed and hung up.

Waiting for Ela had always made me uneasy.
I'd get restless, agitated—
and she was always late.

"I'm coming," she'd say—
then hours would pass.

I lay down on the floor mattress, smoking, waiting.

Maybe an hour later,
she came through the door, arms full of plastic bags.
She had bought seven or eight beers.

We started drinking right away.

I didn't feel like having sex,
and if I didn't feel like it, she usually didn't either.

She was sitting cross-legged,
holding her cigarette loosely between her fingers,
telling stories about what had happened at the site.

I listened, I reacted,
but I didn't really want to hear it.

Her other hand rested lightly on a fat Efes beer bottle
between her legs.
She was wearing a brown leather jacket and black pants.
She looked beautiful.

How thin her hair was.
Was I in love with her?
Did I even know what love was?

Why did we want to get married?

We didn't talk about it much,
but we wanted it—

to normalize ourselves,
to validate our lives.

"Are you hungry, love?"

"A little. You?"

"I'm hungry too.
What should we eat?"

"Ocakbaşı?"

"No way. Too heavy."

"Maybe something at home?"

"I don't know."

"Should we just not eat?"

We laughed.

I had two more beers,
but for some reason,
I wanted to fight.

"Come on, decide something, I'm starving," I said harshly.

Ela looked at me, shocked.
"Why do I always have to decide?
Why is it always me picking where to eat, when to have sex, what to do?
Don't you have your own desires, your own decisions?

And when everything goes wrong,
it all falls on me."

Her face had changed.
She was drinking her beer faster,
talking and talking.

But there was nothing left to say.
We didn't even know what we were fighting about
anymore.

We had deepened the tension without even knowing why.

Finally, Ela finished her beer and said,
"I have to go home.
My parents are waiting."

"Yeah, go.
Run off and leave me behind.
Just like always.
Go back to your warm house,
your safe family.
Leave me here to rot—like always.
Go!"

Ela didn't say,
"I'll stay."
She didn't try to soothe me with sweet words.

She grabbed her bag,
said,

"Goodbye,"
and left.

68

I felt relieved.
I *wanted* to be alone.
I *wanted* to tear down this system of resentment and suffocation—
this life of guarding our interests, maintaining our positions,
and seeking happiness by pleasing others.

My head was pounding.
Taking a break from beer hadn't helped.
The drunkenness had given way to pure pain.

I didn't want to start drinking again.
But I didn't know what else to do.

How had I become so good at abandoning myself like this?
I couldn't hold onto anyone.
I couldn't let anyone hold onto me.

I didn't want to die.
I didn't want to end my life.
I just wanted to *liquidate* it.
To *end* it so I could start over.

I had to begin with that cursed house in Cihangir—
and with Deniz.

I went inside and lay down on the floor mattress.
I had a plan.
I pulled the blanket over myself and tried to sleep.

The plan needed time.
I had to wait for the middle of the night.

My headache put me to sleep...
And my headache woke me again.

Spring had turned up the volume of the street outside.
Through the open window came bright, lively sounds.

I had probably slept no more than an hour.

The breath of the night air smelled sweet,
so much better than the stifling smell of the house.

I got up, dressed quickly without thinking too much.
I was starving.

The beer, the green plums, the tobacco had scorched my stomach raw.

I didn't know what I wanted to eat.
I didn't know what I was craving.
I just walked out into the night.

69

The Same Streets

I kept wandering the same streets,
going in circles,
like a maze that always led me back to the same spot.

A maze built with walls, each one offering a door of escape—
yet the thought of using one of those doors never even crossed my mind.
This was where I felt safe.

What was behind those doors?
I didn't know.
Maybe nothingness.
Maybe annihilation.

So I kept turning, turning, inside the same labyrinth.

My feet carried me without will,
without destination.
Indecision.
Ignorance.

They were taking me to Parmakkapı Sokak.
I passed by the ocakbaşı.
I didn't feel like it.

Parmakkapı Sokak was always a kind of escape.
There was Hayal Kahvesi.

I never liked it.
Rarely went.
It was full of half-intellectual, half-pretentious types.
Not my kind of place.

But just down the street, there was Beyoğlu's first dürümcü.
Cheap.
Good lahmacun.
Always open.

Once, when I was very drunk,
I had eaten an "adana inside lahmacun" here.
Everything inside everything.
The perfect form of life.

When I reached the dürümcü, I turned back.
I didn't feel like eating something with onions.

Across from Hayal Kahvesi, there was a beer hall.
I rarely went there either.
But tonight I went in.

I ordered fries and a beer.
And watched the people passing in the streets.

There was no way out.
I could see it clearly.

Maze above hatred.
Hatred between boredom.
Boredom above monotony.

No way out.

No plan,
no tactic.
I was just going to vanish.
Fade into dust, into the earth...

They said,
"He doesn't even have a place to sleep."
I never understood what that meant—
until now.

I ate the fries quickly, with plenty of ketchup.
Ordered another beer and more fries.
Asked for some bread too.

I ate the second plate with the bread, with ketchup again.
I was full now.

Another beer.

My pains were fading,
but my drunkenness was growing.

Time...

Time refused to pass.
It was 11:30 PM.
A spring night in Istanbul.
Everything, everyone, felt prostituted.

Why didn't I just make peace with that nice little house in Cihangir?
What was my problem?

Just go lie down, man.
Tablecloths, forks and knives, wine glasses, kitchen stuff, bath mats, perfumed soaps, scented candles, burning incense...
Go lie down, what's wrong with you?

Go home, brother.

When I left the beer hall, my feet kept walking aimlessly.
I didn't want to stray far from home.

From Parmakkapı, I walked up to İstiklal.

The crowd had exploded.

So many women, all kinds.
Plenty of men too, maybe even more—
but they didn't interest me.

We were too many.

I couldn't stand İstiklal for long.
I turned down Sadri Alışık and headed for my street.

Should I go to Babybon?
Whisper an "Ah, Marina"?

No, no.
The best was the nameless bar between Bonbon and Babybon.

There, I could lose time.
Time-bar.
Bar-time.

12:15 AM.
I entered the nameless black bar.

I was soaked in beer already.
I ordered a double whiskey with lots of ice.

Tried to drink slowly.
I was drunk now.
Just standing at the bar.
Just standing.

2:15 AM.
I walked out.

70

I still don't know what to do.
Should I go back to the crumbling old house,
or head to Cihangir?

There's nothing in the old house anyway.
Best to go to Cihangir.

I walk down through Çukurcuma toward Cihangir.
The closer I get, the more my chest tightens—
but it's my home, after all.

At least my pajamas are there,
at least my clean clothes are there.

As I approach the building, I see no lights on.
Maybe she's gone to bed,
maybe she's not home at all.

I slip quietly into the building,
turn the key in the lock silently and slowly.

Only the hallway light is on—
that's her habit when she's home alone.

I head to the bathroom first.
The black ceramic tiles
grate on my nerves.

My hatred for the house
—and for Deniz—
surfaces again.

Though I loved Deniz once,
maybe still loved her a little...

But the devils of this house,
they had gotten into her too.

I head to my room.
I don't feel like lying down.

I just stand there.

71

I wander around the apartment.
I open the fridge in the kitchen — almost empty.
Half a bottle of wine with the cork shoved back in, a piece of white cheese, two tomatoes.
I walk into the living room. Everything is still in its place.
I leave the lights on.
I think about going to my room, but my feet hesitate.

Passing by Deniz's door, I stop.
The corridor light spills into her room.
She's lying face down, curled up like a child, still and defenseless.
For a moment, I just stand there, breathing shallowly.
A strange tension swells inside me — not desire, not love, something darker: a desperate hunger for presence, for warmth, for meaning.

I want to step closer.
Not to touch.
Just to exist near her.

The scent of her — of the room, of sleep — reaches me.
It's a pull and a warning at once.
And in that second, I understand: I belong nowhere.
Not to this woman.

Not to this house.
Not to this city.

I breathe out sharply.
Mutter a curse under my breath.
And turn back.

I walk to my room.
I can't bear to stay any longer.
I grab my half-packed suitcase and shove everything into it
— clean, dirty, whatever.
The air of the apartment feels heavier with every second.
I glance back once, toward her door.

Still asleep.

Still far away.

Still unreachable.

I snap the suitcase shut.
Pull the door closed behind me as quietly as I can.

And step into the cold, damp night of Cihangir.

Only one sentence echoes in my mind as I walk away:
"Not if you asked me to stay. Not if you begged me to forgive you."

This time, I'm really leaving.

72

I never went back to that house.
I didn't even go back for the few things I had left behind —
not even the mattress I had dragged in with so much trouble.

Fear, anxiety, guilt...
They ruled the days that followed.

Outwardly, I was calm, quiet.
I barely drank anymore.
But inside, the storm hadn't passed.
Deniz knew Ela. She knew Ahmet.
We had so many mutual friends.
She could easily ruin me if she wanted to, could tell them everything, could shame me completely.

I didn't think she would take it to the police, no — but even that small possibility gnawed at me.
In my own conscience, I was somewhat at peace.
I didn't see it as a pure act of violence — not in the simple way people love to label things.
Not pure rape, not pure consent.
Something else.
A collision. A final reckoning.
An ending.

Still, the guilt stayed with me.
And the leftover paranoia from the endless drinking, the sleepless nights, the remnants of alcohol still burning

through my veins, deepened everything.
Made everything darker. Heavier.

I tried to throw myself into the work at the construction site, but even there — chaos ruled.
I wanted to leave.
I wanted to run.
But somewhere inside, a voice kept whispering:

"Hold on, brother. Finish the job. Put it on your resumé. Build your reputation. Protect your position. Stay strong."

And another voice, louder, angrier:

"Let it all burn. Let them drown in their own filth. Get out, brother. Get out while you can."

And then there was Ela.
If I left, she would stay.
And if she stayed, I would have abandoned her.
Ahmet — he couldn't just walk away either.
Not yet.
He had his own battles with the bosses, his own silent wars.
Eventually, he would leave too.
But not now.
Not yet.

If I left first, they would talk.
They were already talking behind my back — I could feel it.
Ela would hear it too, but she wouldn't tell me.
And her silence would fester between us.

Grow into anger.
Grow into shame.

I needed to be strong.

Or maybe...
I needed to give in completely.

73

Ela was pleased with my calm and quiet mood, but the fact that I wasn't drinking anymore unsettled her a little. We had started talking seriously about marriage. We were also beginning to think about moving into a cleaner apartment near the old house, believing we would stay in this job longer. It made sense — while we still had access to construction workers and materials, we could fix up a place to actually live in. This idea tied me a little more to the job. Ela and Ahmet had found it strange that I had left the Cihangir house so suddenly, but we hadn't talked about it at length. I had just said, *"The rent was too high, Deniz wanted to bring in two more roommates, and when they had to move in urgently, I decided to move back to the old place."* It was a good cover story.

One evening, while I was heading home, the antique dealer downstairs came up to me.
"Brother, someone left something for you," he said.
It was a large black garbage bag. Inside were my remaining belongings from Cihangir. It was double-bagged because of the weight.
"Who left it?" I asked.

"Short red-haired girl," he said.
It was Deniz. So, she had forgiven me, in a way.
"Thanks," I said, and hauled the bag upstairs.
I stuffed everything inside straight into the washing machine and set it running.
I had become more attentive to housework and cleaning now. I was cooking for myself. I had started reading again. I even began scribbling things in Ahmet's old notebooks — some poems, some short stories.

After taking a shower and changing clothes, I set pots of water for pasta and tea on the stove. In the living room, I had built a little order on the dining table with books and notebooks. I had bought all kinds of pens. I felt like someone else. I had been purified somehow — clean.
No problems.
I had made pasta with cheese. It almost tasted like börek. It went well with tea. I was eating while working at the table. I was writing a story. A little bit about myself, a little bit about another.
Is there really a story that is not a little bit about oneself?

74

That evening, Ela called. She was home, in Göztepe. We chatted a bit. A typical lovers' conversation. Words of love and affection. *My dear, my love, my sweetheart.* I wasn't very good at it, but I let myself go. I pulled someone out of the *me-catalog*, someone else, and spoke as them.
Then I'd sit at the table and become someone else again.
I'd go down to the corner store, buy two beers, and once again become someone else.

Sometimes, two beers didn't amount to much.
But they sped up my writing.
I lit my cigarette like someone else.
I wasn't *me* anymore.
I couldn't recognize myself.

On the radio, a classical piece was playing — its rhythm unsettled me — but I didn't change it.
I wanted to keep the tension inside me alive.
I wanted to keep the little irritants of the moment simmering…

While I was lost in a poem, I heard a slight noise at the door. Not a knock — just a sound, as if someone had come and gone.
I didn't pay much attention.
I went on with what I was doing.
Then I started to feel uneasy.
I got up — partly to use the toilet, partly to check the door.
There was an envelope on the floor, clearly slipped under the door.
A small white envelope, with my name on it.
When I picked it up, I realized it wasn't an envelope — just a card, folded in half.

I opened the card.
In the corner was an image of a red carnation, curved like a crescent.
In elegant, delicate handwriting, it read:

"I missed you.
Come to Bonbon after midnight.

I'll be waiting."
MARINA

...

75

I entered Bonbon around 2:00 a.m.
The best hour of the night — not too early, not too late.
You're not stuck sitting around anxiously waiting for something to happen, nor are you caught in the panic of "the night's ending, I need to do something."
Though, tonight, my purpose was different.
I was there for a meeting, a rendezvous — I had been summoned.

The club staff welcomed me with great respect — even affection — enough to make me feel like the guest of honor for the night.
Without asking anything, they led me straight to a private booth they had reserved at the back.
The head waiter asked how I was, then disappeared without even asking what I'd like to drink.
Almost immediately, a tray arrived with a bottle of rakı, mezes, and all the fixings.
Rakı, water, and ice — all perfectly chilled.

I asked the head waiter for cigarettes, and also for a soda with lemon — and extra lemons on the side.
I wanted to *crush* the rakı tonight, dilute it, sip it slow and steady.

The bill would break my back, sure, but my spirits were high.

Marina wasn't anywhere in sight.
And I couldn't bring myself to ask about her.

Since I hadn't been drinking much in recent days, I finished my first glass too fast — the speed stripping away the slow anxiety of waiting.
By the second round, I slowed down, nibbling on the mezes.

My eyes kept scanning for Marina.
There were lots of girls at Bonbon that night.
Then, a woman appeared from near the stage, chatting with a group of girls standing by a table.
She was wearing tight jeans, serious heels, and a short leather jacket.
She didn't look like one of the regulars who worked there.
More like a businesswoman, someone who'd gone shopping on a Saturday afternoon.

She was heading toward me.
She looked like Marina — but she wasn't limping.
Her hair was shorter now, and dyed black.
She carried a small handbag.

She came up to me and sat down.
"You don't recognize me, do you, darling?" she said.

It was Marina.

"I do, I do," was all I could manage to say.

76

- "But you — you've changed. You're not limping anymore." (I was stunned.)
- "Yes. It was all an act, a game I played to stay unnoticed. A bit cruel, maybe, but... necessary."
- "But why?"
- "Partly to get to know you. Partly because of my routine assignment. You know, I explained it at the hotel. Because of my covert mission…"
- "Why did you want to get to know me? Why me?"
- "You were chosen. Maybe long before me, even before you were born. I just came to find you."
- "But chosen for what?"
- "That I can't tell you. You have to find out."
- "How am I supposed to find out?"
- "Don't ask too many questions about that right now. Come on, let's drink… Cheers."
- "Cheers."
- …
- …
- "How well do you know me?"
- "Better than you think. We know all your relationships."
- "All of them?" (I was curious...)
- "Yes, all of them."
- "Even the Gypsy girl, Afet — you know about her too?"
- "Of course. She's one of us. Yes, she's ours too."
- "Off..."

- "We know about Deniz and Ela too."
- "Are they part of your circle too?"
- "No, but a friend of Deniz's works with us. She tells us everything."
- "Everything?" (I was getting uneasy.)
- "Everything." (She smiled mischievously, almost mocking me.)
- "And... (I hesitated) that night? Did she tell about *that night* too?" (I was tense.)
- "Which night?" (Marina laughed at the state I was in.)
- "That night... and if she did, how did she tell it?"
- "Look, it's not a problem. She didn't make it a big deal. In fact, she expected it from you. She was sad when you left... But it's good you did. You needed to leave that place. I'm glad. Some spaces don't bring us luck — they can even curse us. That house was bad for you... But this house you're in now, it isn't right for you either."
- "Then what should I do?"
- "We'll find you a new place. Nearby. Tomorrow an agent will call you, he'll show you a spot a few streets down. Take it. Fix it up a little. Just like you and Ela planned. It'll be a center — a library, both for you and for us."
- "Alright, I'll take it. But what about work? The consulate job is killing me. I want to run away."
- "I know. Hold on a little longer. Get the place, fix it up, set up the library. Then you can resign..."
- "And Ela?"

- "Ela's a good girl. In time, you'll explain things to her. About us. About the real situation."
- "But I'm confused… What exactly are we trying to do? What's the goal?"
- "Don't worry about that now. It will reveal itself in time…"
- "Why am I drinking so much?"
- "The alcohol is protecting your mind. It shields you from the cosmic and spiritual attacks directed at you. That's why you *have* to drink — for now. But soon, you won't need it anymore. Relax. Cheers — to us and to what we are building…"
- "Will you come home with me tonight?"
- (Laughing) "No, not tonight. Tonight is business."
- "Alright… Does it bother you that I've been with different women?"
- "No. Why should it? That's why you're important. These are the limits drawn by the State, by society, even by the so-called divine order. We're against all rigid relationship forms. We stand for love, for choosing and living freely. Sex liberates humanity — that's why they try to control it. The so-called sexual liberation since the '70s only created a market and a degraded future society. You're caught in it, but you're still different."
- (I was stunned — truly stunned.) "And what about Afet?"
- "As I said, she's with us too. She may come and go, she might bring you messages. You can trust her."

We had emptied the rakı bottle.
Marina drank like water — no sign of drunkenness.

I, on the other hand, was reeling — not from the rakı, but from her words, from *her*.

I was signaling to call for the bill when Marina caught my arm and lowered it.

"No more bills for you here. You've already paid enough," she said.
"Who's paying then, you?" I asked.
"Don't worry about it. This place is practically ours," she said, giving me a quick kiss on the lips.

Then she stood up.
I drained my last sip and followed her out into the night.

77

The New Apartment...

The apartment the agent showed me was on Yadigâr Street, just a block down from Turnacıbaşı. Below it, a newly opened antique shop had just set up — but for an antique shop, it was nearly empty, just a few large pieces of furniture scattered around. The apartment was on the second floor. It had high ceilings and tall doors. The window frames had been recently renovated — and that was the most important thing. It only needed a fresh coat of paint.

You entered the apartment into a spacious hall. Immediately to the left, a small corridor branched off, leading to two doors — one for the bathroom, the other for the kitchen. Continuing straight from the hall, you reached a wide living room, and on the left, through a pair of large glass-paneled double doors, there was another room. That inner room got its light only through the glass doors.

I was already planning in my head.
I would put a floor mattress and a wardrobe in the small room — that would be the sleeping room, for me and Ela. Or simply, the "bedroom."
On the right side of the entrance hall, there would be two rows of bookshelves — one against the wall, the other freestanding in the middle.
The shelves would continue into the living room.
Two desks and a three-seater couch would complete the space.
The living room would be the main workspace, the heart of our cell.

That was it.
The conditions and the rent were a little steep, but Marina had said, "Don't worry about the money."

I told the agent, "I'd like to show it to my fiancée tonight before making a final decision."
We agreed to meet again at 7:00 PM.
I liked the place.

At the site, I couldn't fully concentrate on work — my mind was wrapped up in the new apartment.
Fortunately, management had failed to vacate and hand over part of the building to us yet, so some of the workers were idle.

I would use them for the renovations.
Now all I could think about was the apartment.
Ela would surely like it too, so I had already started organizing workers and materials for the next day.

I had told Ela that it was intended as a "home office," so she wouldn't question the setup — at least until the time was right to explain everything.

I couldn't bear the hours at the construction site that day.
At one point, I slipped out and went to Asmalımescit.
There was a small spot next to Refik's place — I knocked back a quick rakı there and returned.
It helped the time pass.

Later, I walked the site again.
In truth, the work was flowing.
After a while, a construction site becomes like a machine — once it's set up, even if you shout "Stop!" it keeps moving on its own.

78

We were in front of the building a little before 7.
The real estate agent hadn't arrived yet.
We went into the antique shop downstairs and browsed around.
The owner came over.
We struck up a conversation.
When he learned we were both architects, he was thrilled.
"Hope you rent it," he said.
The shop really was empty — they had just finished the

renovation, and they were still moving in pieces from their other location down in Çukurcuma.
Right in the middle of our chat, the agent showed up — he must have seen us inside.

We went upstairs immediately.
I just wanted to wrap it up quickly.
Ela walked around the place carefully, tiptoeing lightly and smiling.
When the agent was distracted for a moment, she leaned in and whispered, "I think it's good."
"I think so too," I said.

That was it. We were taking it.

Everyone was happy.
I had brought the deposit with me, handed it over.
The agent gave me the keys.
"We know you, we trust you," he said.

Ela asked,
"Where do they know you from?"
"Friends of Bahadır's," I said, brushing it off.

Once the agent left, Ela threw her arms around my neck, practically shouting,
"I love it! I love it so much!"
She had already started dreaming about the place.
I gently reminded her that it was going to be a "home-office," a library.

"Well, whatever," she said, a little deflated,
"At least it's ours."

She hadn't loved the home-office idea.
She was a little hurt.
To soften the mood, I said,
"Come on, let's go to Refik's and celebrate."

"Refik's is a little far. Let's go to Nevizade, to İmroz," she said.

I agreed.
Tonight, whatever she wanted.

At İmroz, my mind was restless.
It felt like a long, drawn-out hangover had been chasing me all day.
Ela noticed.
"Are you sick or something?" she asked.

I wasn't.
But the same undefined distance — and the magnetism we couldn't quit — sat heavily between us again.
When I looked at her, I didn't see my missing half.
I had never seen that.
But I did see a reflection of myself.

How was I going to tell her all this?
That the house was going to be a cell — a very closed, secretive cell.
Marina placed huge importance on privacy.
"Think of it like a religious household," she had said.

Nobody from outside the cell should see in.
Otherwise, Marina believed, the "blessing" would be broken.
Nobody could even see the books.
The books were our weapons, carrying us into the future.
Books in different languages, in different colors...

We didn't stay long at İmroz.
We went back to the house early.
Ela was going to stay over — she hadn't in a while.
Had I missed her?
I wasn't sure.
Maybe I missed Marina more.
But Marina had said, "Spread love."
It didn't matter.
We were all fragments of one great body:
Ela, Marina, Afet, Deniz...
It was all the same — love, for us, was a dialectical sum.

These were our last nights in the old house.
It was one of those rare places where you could actually feel a bond with the walls.
I knew I would miss it when I left.
But there was no other way.

"You're a nomad," Marina had said.
And I had only just begun to migrate.

That night, Ela and I were like an old married couple.
We each took a shower separately, wrapped ourselves in towels, and lay side by side.

We kissed for a long time, made love slowly, without changing positions much…

79

The next day, renovations were starting at the new house.
The workers were going to come directly to the house.
I would head straight there too, to open the door for them and get them started.
Ela would go to the construction site.

The workers arrived looking a little uneasy.
Once inside, they changed into their overalls — they had brought them along in plastic bags.
I explained the job: it was a simple paint and plastering job.
Only, there was serious scraping work to do on the walls — the plaster had rotted.

"This scraping will take all day," we agreed.

As the scraping began, dust filled the air.
The workers hadn't brought dust masks.
They tied rags around their mouths, whatever they could find, to shield themselves.
You could barely see anything — a thick white fog — and it made me sad.

"I'll bring you real masks from the site at noon," I said and left.

I didn't want to see people.
So I decided to loop around the back of Galatasaray High

School, heading for the quiet street between the school and the Yapı Kredi building.
The back streets were empty, calm, silent.
A few stragglers walked by.
A cool breeze brushed my face.

Behind Galatasaray's back courtyard, there was a small slope — a forgotten scrap of nature.
I always slowed down there.
I wanted to soak it in a little longer.

When I reached the side street by Galatasaray, I crossed over and walked along the buildings.
There were more people now.
When I hit İstiklal, I crossed it and turned left at the British Consulate.
This alley was lined with empty, abandoned buildings.
Then came Tepebaşı, the front of the Büyük Londra Hotel, and Pera Palace — and then the Consulate.

I had arrived.

I had arrived at the one place I didn't want to be.

When I entered the office, it felt like everyone was against me — or maybe I was just imagining it.
Was I losing my place here?
Was my image as the brilliant, hardworking, stubborn young chief falling apart?

I went straight down to Ela's room, where I usually worked now too.

"So how's it going at the house?" she asked, her eyes still on the computer screen.

"Good. We started, but the plaster's bad. We're scraping. Let's see how long it takes."

"Ahmet, Birol, and some others from the office are coming tomorrow," Ela said casually, scrolling.

I was surprised.
News like this usually came to me first.
I guess I really wasn't the center anymore.

"When did you hear about this?" I asked.

"Well, they called me last night after work, but I forgot to tell you with everything about the house and all," she said.

I was angry, but I hid it.
How could you forget something like that?
"Typical woman's mind," I thought to myself.

"Did they say why they're coming?"

"I don't know exactly — probably got called by management."

The picture was becoming clear.
A crisis meeting.
An announcement of my failure.

But why was I even bothering?
I already wanted to leave.

I had bigger things to focus on now — we had bigger things.

I thought about calling Ahmet, but decided to wait until the afternoon.

"Anyway, I'm going out to the field," I said, putting on my hardhat and leaving.

Ela could tell I was upset.
She knew me.

First I went to the warehouse and ordered six dust masks to be dropped at my desk.
Then I headed into the building.
The large hall we hadn't yet taken possession of was finally being cleared.
This was the main battle zone.
Soon it would be ours — but first, demolition.
The steel partition walls were still there.
These walls divided inside from outside for visa applicants — thick walls, made of double 10mm steel sheets.

There would be a lot of scrap metal — a good payday for the contractor.

I stayed out on the field until noon.
Being around the workers, explaining things, relaxed me.
It made the job bearable — a kind of therapy.

When I returned to the office, the white bag of dust masks was already sitting on my desk.
I grabbed it.

"I'm going to the new house," I told Ela.
I didn't want her to come with me, for some reason.

I rushed out of the consulate.
This time, I went up to İstiklal by cutting through the side of the Oda Kule building.

80

At the house, the scraping work was still going on.
When I entered, the workers paused.
The foreman came over to me.
I moved into the kitchen — there was no scraping happening there, it was a place where you could actually talk.

"Boss, this job's getting bigger," he said. "The more we scrape, the more comes off. There's no solid base, it's all the same. If it keeps going like this, we'll end up scraping the whole place."

I thought for a moment.
"What do you think we should do?"

"Boss, maybe we could try a primer, but it won't hold on this dusty, rotten plaster. There's no cement left, it's all crumbling. I don't know, boss, what can we even do?"

The idea of primer was good — it sparked something in my mind.

"What if we used glue?" I said. "Cheap white glue, brushed onto the walls — it would harden and hold the plaster together."

The foreman thought about it.

"Let's try it, boss," he said.

"Alright. Stop scraping for now. Let the dust settle. Wipe the walls down with wet brushes. I'll send you some glue this afternoon — and maybe a can of primer too. Mix it together and apply it."

"Okay, boss," he said.

I left.
I immediately went back to the old house.
I wanted to stretch my lunch break — I didn't want to go back to the site.
I needed to deliver the payment certificates.
I hated the payment work, but that's what everything — all the effort, all these people — was about.
To "earn" it.
To get what we were "owed."
But was this really what we deserved?

I lay down on the couch and lit a cigarette.
I loved the darkness of this house, its dimness.
It made the world feel like I didn't exist.

When I was here, it was a comforting thought — that I was invisible.

Where was Marina now, I wondered?
When would she touch me again — not just my body, but my mind?

It was her touch on my mind that I loved most.
Maybe that's why I followed her like I was under a spell.
Whatever she said, I obeyed.

I closed my eyes and started drifting into daydreams.
I imagined: *If the door knocked now and Marina walked in...*
No.
Not Marina.
Marina belonged to the night.

If the door knocked now, and the gypsy girl, Afet, walked in...
I barely knew her, but somehow it made sense.
Yes — Marina had said Afet was "one of us," and she would likely become a member of our cell.

I got up and put a CD into the player:

Dmitri Shostakovich (1906–1975)
Symphony No. 7 in C major, Op. 60 "Leningrad"
Valery Gergiev
Mariinsky Theatre Orchestra
Konzerthaus, Vienna, 4 December 2010

81

I lay back and closed my eyes.
Yes, loneliness was not a natural state for a human being —
but at our core, we were always alone.
I was drifting away.
It felt like a fatal sleep, a breath-stealing sleep.
The music was carrying me elsewhere, its melodies
building obstacles across the runaway currents of my mind
— leading me along a pebbled path by a riverbank.
I was stumbling.
My ankles twisting, my knees buckling — it was so hard to
walk here.
If only I could fall into the river, drift downward, all the
way to the sea, reach a delta...
Mud and dirt, stone and organic debris covering me...
I could smell the sea, the salt in the air.
My body brushed against soft underwater moss, I was
swimming with the fish,
floating in an endless white sea.

I just smiled...
Frozen in time, suspended — alone, singular.

I heard a noise, a soft tapping — like someone was
knocking at the door, insistently but gently.
A "Let me in, I'm here" kind of knock.
If only I could wake up, I would open the door.
But I couldn't climb out of this sleep, out of this sea.
Following my grandmother's old trick, I shook my right
ankle slightly —

A jolt ran through my body —
I was finally starting to wake up…

The knocking continued.
I stood up and went to open the door:

THE GYPSY GIRL, AFET.

She entered without a word.
We lay down together on the floor mattress —
as if we had done this a thousand times before, knowingly, familiarly.

Our hands brushed.
A bony, rough hand.
There was a damp, earthy smell coming from her body —
like she had just bathed in the very river I'd dreamed of,
and her clothes had dried on her skin.
That raw, primal scent.

I turned toward her, leaning my body partly against hers.
She turned her face to me, gazing with large, dark eyes.
Neither soft nor harsh —
a little mercy, a little cruelty.
She was looking at me as if she were looking at herself.

I placed my left hand just below her belly.
I was trembling with excitement — too overwhelmed even to make love.

- "What's your name, your real name?" I asked.
- "Afet. You call me Afet — that's my name now."

- "But that's the name I gave you, isn't it? That's not your real name."
- "It became real. Marina calls me Afet too now. That's my code name in the cell."

(We both smiled. My left hand wandered over Afet's body. It felt like touching a part of myself — that close.)

- "Then what's my name?" I asked. "I never told you. Do I have a name or a code name?"
- "No. You have no name, brother. I'll just call you 'Abi.' You won't have a name in this cell."
- "Did Marina tell you that?"
- "Yes. But even if she hadn't, that's how it should be."
- "What's your role in the cell then? Do you know?"
- "Roles shift. They're not fixed. For example, today I'm here on an assignment."
- "What kind of assignment?"
- "To take you and lead you to another cell."
- "Why?"
- "It's a kind of initiation. Something you need to see."
- "Did Marina arrange it?"
- "For now, she arranges everything in this cell."
- "But I need to go back to the site…"
- "Don't worry about it. Sister Ela will cover for you..."
- "Does she know I won't be coming?"
- "The message has reached her. Relax."
- "Should we go now?"
- "Yes, let's go."

(Music from the stereo was still playing.
I asked — half as a joke —)

- "Do you know who's playing?"
- "Of course. Shostakovich. Symphony No. 7."
- "No time for making love?"
- "Not this time," *(she said with a laugh)*, "But I'll be back...
  And we'll talk for a long, long time."

82

Afet was walking a little ahead.
That was the plan.
I had no idea where we were going — I was simply following her.
Two barefoot, scrawny girls and a bald-headed boy had joined her — that was her gang.

Once Afet stepped out of the house, she changed.
She became herself again — the swaggering, cursing Gypsy girl.
We climbed up from Sadri Alışık Street.
The bouncers outside the bars and nightclubs, the policemen standing guard at the station, the shopkeepers — everyone greeted Afet or catcalled her.
I followed behind.
She was walking quickly.

Once we crossed Sadri Alışık and then İstiklal, we pressed on, crossing the boulevard too.
We were heading into Tarlabaşı.

Passing by the building where the laborers stayed made me uneasy.
Here, Afet was even more at ease with the crowd.
She even playfully pushed and shoved a few men, laughing.
During those moments, I would slow my steps —
the street ignored me completely, treating me as if I wasn't there.
I felt like I was wandering through a movie set.

But I didn't feel threatened.
Passing the laborers' building, we slipped deeper into the backstreets.
The atmosphere changed — it grew quieter but more marginal, rougher.
I completely lost my sense of direction.
Was the sea to my left? Was İstiklal behind me?
I had no idea.

Were we walking in circles?
Were these ruins all blending together into one?
I didn't know anymore.

Afet and the kids finally stopped in front of a building —
only the skeletal frame remained.
A few seconds later, the children disappeared.
Afet was waiting for me.
As I reached her, I noticed the inside of the skeletal structure was covered in ivy.

"Come," she said, moving toward the entrance.
There was no door — it looked like the mouth of a cave.

We pushed through the hanging ivy.
Behind it, there was just enough space for a person to pass.
At the center of the clearing stood a structure — painted in mottled shades of green and brown like a tree — two stories tall, with a window on each side.
The windows were black, mirrored glass.
The reflections of the ivy made it look like there were no windows at all — creating a complete illusion.

At the center, there was a door, painted the same way.
Afet knocked once and the door opened immediately.
Inside was a single open space —
only a bright red steel staircase on the far wall led to the upper floor.

The four walls, aside from the window spaces, were completely lined with shelves — packed full of books.
There wasn't room for a single more.

Following Afet, we climbed upstairs.
The second floor was arranged the same way, but at the center stood a large oval table, like a meeting table.
One of the shelves was empty.
Across its front, large letters read: **"PROTECT YOUR CELL."**

Afet sat down in one of the chairs by the table.
"We have time," she said.
"You can look at the books."

It was the first time I found myself alone with Afet and didn't feel like touching her.

It was a blank, white cell.
The presence of all these books made even touching myself seem unnecessary.

The arrangement of the books was chaotic —
different languages, different subjects, stacked side-by-side, sometimes even piled on top of each other so tightly that pulling one book might topple them all.

There was mostly Turkish —
but also Kurdish, English, Romanian, Russian, German, Arabic, Farsi, and other languages I couldn't even identify.

All subjects —
but especially history, art, poetry, novels, essays…

Unable to resist, I asked:

- "What is this place?"
- "It's a kind of sanctuary," she said.
  "We call it the central cell. A meeting place. A center for gathering."

I didn't want to ask too many questions — afraid to shatter the spell of the moment.

- "Can I go downstairs?" I asked.
- "Of course," she said.

I went back down.
I started wandering along the shelves.
It was a mesmerizing collection —

a brotherhood of books, where opposites sat side by side as
if they had always belonged together.
You could sense it wasn't random —
there was an invisible order, you just had to look deeper,
tilt your head, look sideways.

I completed my slow circle of the room and returned to the
stairs.
Upstairs, I walked slowly along the shelves again.
It felt like a kind of **tawaf** — a sacred cosmic orbit.

I was especially drawn to the books whose languages I
couldn't understand.
They seemed to hide endless, bottomless secrets.

I hadn't dared pull out a single book.
If I touched one, I felt like all would collapse.

These books were meant to stay together —
holding some meaning just in their arrangement.

When I reached the stairs again, I turned to look at Afet.
She was waiting patiently at the table, giving a small nod
for me to join her.

I sat down across from her.
Only now could I truly perceive the form of the table —
it wasn't a circle, it wasn't an oval.
It had no beginning or end —
everyone sat in equal place around it.
It gave the illusion of spinning, changing — but it was
peaceful, like a dervish turning under the sky.

I lifted my head.
Above us, light streamed through a sliced glass dome —
you could just make out the outer boundaries of the
building.

There was no need for words.
Afet and I sat in silence.

I don't know how long we waited —
we entered a kind of trance.

Then we heard the downstairs door open.

Afet looked at me and said,
"They're here."

Three people came up the stairs.

I started to rise, but Afet signaled gently for me to stay
seated.

The three sat down at the table.
One was Marina —
seeing her filled me with relief and a quiet smile.
The second was clearly a transgender woman.
The third was a mustached, dark-skinned man who looked
unmistakably from the East.

For a while, none of us spoke.

Then Marina started speaking —
but at certain points, without any break or hesitation, the

transgender woman continued the sentence,
and then the mustached man picked it up seamlessly.

Their speech flowed from mouth to mouth.

The essence of what they said was:

83

"You know why we brought you here.
This is not an initiation ceremony into a religious order or a Masonic lodge.
It cannot be — because we have no rules.

No matter how many rules we might try to create,
no matter what we might try to write down,
it would always fall short,
or it would end up restricting the freedoms of you, of us, or of others.

That's why, in this sanctuary,
with these books,
we symbolize that we are in the eternal service of infinite knowledge, wisdom, and mind.

We believe in the material and spiritual accumulation of centuries, millennia, millions of years.
So many words have been spoken.
So much has been written.
And yet, the world remains the same.

No concept has been produced that could truly change it at the root.
Everything that exists is built upon flawed practices.

We reject this —
we reject all so-called truths.

That's why we say nothing.
Now, it no longer matters **what** someone says or **how true** it is.
What matters is **who** says it, **why** they say it, and **for whom** they say it.

This is where the slavery of knowledge begins.
We reject the slavery of knowledge.

We reject all modern and traditional institutions.
We reject all models and tools of change.
We reject all tools and models of production.
We reject all forms of ownership and existence.
We reject all modern and traditional forms of sentiment and mediation.
We reject every way of being, every imposed style of existence that has been forced upon us.

We have only three principles:

1. This is a brotherhood, a fellowship.
2. Change and transformation are endless. Truths exist within that endlessness.

3. The principle written on every cell's wall:
   PROTECT YOUR CELL —
   in the name of our loyalty and our continuity.

Welcome among us!"

84

The next day, Ahmet and Birol's visit — just as I had
expected — was a clear signal of some kind of operation.
Ahmet, with his usual sincere demeanor, smiled at me kindly,
while Birol launched his sharp, needling questions,
demanding explanations.

Even though I was still partly under the spell of the previous day,
Birol's attitude was affecting me.
He was playing at being the boss, judging on his own
terms, ready to convict.
No matter how much I told myself, *"I don't care,"*
I did care.

What gnawed at me was my sense of responsibility.
No matter what, I couldn't convince myself that I had the
right to misuse other people's resources and time.
I should have known that everything happening around me
— this entire environment — was wrong from the start.
Maybe it was childishness on my part, maybe naïveté,
but that's who I was, and it was eating me alive inside.

During the site visit, tensions almost snapped.
It was only through Ahmet's mediation that the conversation continued at all.
All the negatives were pinned on me,
yet none of the positives were even mentioned.

It was starting to burn inside me...
I was on the verge of walking away, quitting right there.
Ahmet noticed, took my arm, and gently pulled me aside,
away from Birol and the group.

That evening, we were all supposed to go out for dinner together.
Ahmet said, "We'll go to Refik or Yakup's."
But I was desperately trying to find an excuse to avoid it.
As the afternoon wore on, around five, I slipped away to the old apartment.

I had paused the renovation at the new place for a day — just until Birol left.
I needed a proper excuse.
Leaving without one would seem too obvious.

Around six, my phone rang — it was Ahmet.
"Where are you, what happened?" he asked.
I mumbled something incoherent.

"Birol's not coming tonight," he said,
"he's with his wife. It'll just be you, me, and Ela. We'll head out in half an hour. Meet us at Refik's."

My spirits lifted instantly.
"Alright," I said.

85

At Refik tavern, Ahmet seemed to be in another world. He wasn't getting into topics about the construction site, Birol, etc. at all. He was talking about establishing a publishing house and starting a magazine. Before this job, he had been the editor of an important art magazine. He was thinking about translating classics that hadn't been translated, and he had many other ideas. Ahmet had clearly put the consulate job out of his mind. After a few doubles, we too had begun to support Ahmet. Ahmet was considering Ela and me as managers for the publishing house. After a while, I couldn't resist asking, "That's all well and good, but what are we going to do about this job, the consulate job?" Ahmet gave a sidelong smile. "This job will end, not much left, don't worry," he said. So it was finished, though physically there was still more to go. The package that was said to be excessive had barely been completed. This business was making me melancholy. Ahmet had again turned the subject to our new plans. Was Ahmet one of us too? I was beginning to suspect...

When we left, we all went to the decrepit house together. Ahmet still, despite months passing, seemed uncomfortable with Ela and me sleeping together. Not that he said anything, but I could tell from the changing expression in his eyes. But I couldn't sleep apart from my girlfriend just because he was uncomfortable...

Being **organized** hadn't made much difference in my life. I couldn't feel any difference. The renovation of the house was finished. I had told the company I would be leaving. Everyone was relieved. I had neither resigned nor been fired; it was ending like a relationship that ends by itself. I had ordered the bookshelves. I had moved my bed and belongings to the new house and was staying there. I had told Ahmet that I had moved out of the house. He hadn't asked for the key, saying, "Keep it, just in case." Ela had loved the house very much, staying with me more often, but Marina and Afet were silent; there was no sound from them. There was no point in going to Bonbon or Babybon without Marina calling. Afet wasn't coming to the old street either. I was thinking of going to the central cell in Tarlabaşı, but I was afraid of not being able to find it. Weeks were passing in a pessimistic, uncertain state...

86

Finally, I had left the job; the inevitable had happened.

Leaving like this, unfinished, didn't sit well with me, but I had no other choice.

Finally, we had also finished the cell house.

The shelves had arrived, and the table too. I had settled in the glazed room. I had placed all my books on the shelves, but they were still very empty. Ela stayed with me as much as she could. She was still working at the consulate. She would stop by after work, go back to her own house late at night, but most of the time she stayed with me. I was usually at home, reading, writing, thinking, passing time.

Afet and Marina weren't making contact, but I missed Afet the most. Because of her youth, her closeness to my age, or her animal attraction... One day, when I went to buy beer from the kiosk near the old house, I had seen her. She had made an eye signal and then followed me. As I entered the house, I had purposely left the downstairs door open; she came ten minutes later. We lay down and chatted in bed; we didn't make love with her anymore for some reason, we just touched. We didn't kiss either. Having her body beside me was enough.

She had brought me information: on Friday night, that is, toward dawn on Saturday at five, Marina would come, and I needed to be alone in the house. Ela usually stayed with me on Fridays, but I would find a way.

87

On Friday, I told Ela I would be meeting Bahadır in the evening. "We have guests anyway, so that works out," she said. I spent the entire day in bed; I had never liked waiting. I slept as much as I could during the day and generally ate at home. Around 3 AM, the door rang. I opened it. It was Marina. She had come early this time. We sat at the table. We were more distant:

- What will we do now?
- Nothing; keeping the cell alive is our primary duty.
- How will this place survive?

- First, we need to fill the shelves with books...
- We need money for books.
- We can't buy books with money.
- What should we do?
- I have an idea. Do you still have the key to the old house?
- Yes, I do.
- There are many books in that house, and almost all of them are good, the kind we collect. Let's take them here.
- How? Steal them?
- Let's not call it stealing, let's say relocating...
- If Ahmet finds out about this, it will be very bad. I can't do this.
- Do it. Don't worry about Ahmet; he won't make a fuss. Starting tomorrow, gradually bring them here in bags; you're already going in and out of the house anyway.
- Okay, I'll start. But what will I tell Ela?
- Tell her, "I spoke with Ahmet, he wanted it." Ela won't call and ask about this.
- Alright. Let's lie down; you must be tired.

88

We opened a beer each and stretched out.
Marina, with the same effortless mastery, stripped and slipped into the bed.
I did the same.
First, we drank our beers.

My mind was in turmoil.
What was I even doing?

When we finished the beer, I kissed Marina, just to stop thinking.
She was so alive, so strong.
Her body responded to every move you made —
her hands would go exactly where you wished they would,
as if they were extensions of your own will.
Always touching the right places, moving at the right rhythms...

Marina stayed until noon the next day.

After she left, I called Ela.
She said she wouldn't be coming over that weekend — she would stop by after work on Monday.
I wanted to start moving the books immediately.
I had to finish by Monday night.

I got dressed and headed out — back to the old house.
There, I found a navy blue sports bag, not even sure who it belonged to.
I started filling it with books from my room's shelves.
Books were heavy — one full bag was about as much as I could carry.

I left and walked over to the new apartment.
I placed the books onto the shelves there.

I had a similar bag at the new place.
I figured if I used both, one on each shoulder, I could carry

more evenly.
After a short rest, I took both bags and returned to the old house.
This time, I filled them again — not quite as full as the first load — but still heavier.
Once more, I carried them over to the new place.
I shelved the books again without resting and immediately went back.

At the old house, I started packing the bags once more.
I was exhausted.
I decided to rest a little at the old place.

I stretched out on the couch in the living room — the same way I had done for months.

After a while, I got up and loaded a Bach CD into the player.
Best of Bach...

89

What was playing sounded like some kind of church music.
I craved a cigarette, alcohol — anything and everything I could find.
There was always something left behind in this house, something forgotten…
I began searching through every drawer, shelf, every little box.
Frantically searching, but finding nothing.

Then, inside the small drawer of the console, I found a piece of paper, folded in four.
At the top, it had my name written on it:

"To love infinitely or scarcely at all... Could you be careful with how you measure me?
Who is better off than whom — like who loves more than whom — can never truly be known.
You must convince me, convince me that if I offer my existence to yours, you will be able to bear it.
Or if I break myself apart, scatter myself across your faith, your path of truth —
that somehow we can become a more whole 'two.'

There is no difference between giving and taking.
Whoever receives remains just as indebted to the giver.

I am far more careful with what you feel than you imagine.
But by disregarding what I myself feel,
I sometimes unconsciously try to make you pay for it —
and that, I call 'a mistake.'

My truth — not something I cling to tightly —
is that I see myself, at once, immensely significant to 'everything'
and yet microscopically insignificant before 'everything.'

Against the evil of the universe,
what has been done to me carries no weight at all.

That is why I cannot understand holding a grudge, and I cannot stand by you if you do.

I am too hesitant even to say 'Change this,'
but among all I have learned, one thing matters to me:

The more you expand yourself, the more awareness you will gain.
The more you allow yourself to grow and shed the small, foolish hooks that cling to you,
the more you will take on a nebular chemistry.

Your presence will stretch wide across the emptiness.
It is to be vast. It is to be beautiful.

And the things that will matter to you will be these.
You will be on a path whose end you cannot see,
and it is precisely because you cannot see its end that you will find the strength to walk it."*

ELA

90

This was a letter that had never reached me —
it must have been written months ago.
I kept reading it over and over, trying to understand.
Or maybe it wasn't that old after all. I didn't know.

Ela must have known everything — that's what the letter meant.
But she loved me, and I had wronged her.

I hadn't shown her enough attention, hadn't taken her seriously enough.
I had been under the influence of other things surrounding me.

On Monday night, I would tell her everything.
The whole truth.
I couldn't live with this lie any longer.
I couldn't do that to someone.

This wasn't just physical betrayal —
this was real betrayal.

I hoisted the bags back onto my shoulders and went again to the new house.
I emptied the books onto the table without even bothering to place them on the shelves properly.
I just wanted to finish.
Without resting, I left again, continuing the hauling.
I wouldn't stop until it was done.
I wanted to be free of it.

Later, I would go out —
there was no way to get through tonight without drinking.

For a moment, I thought about going over to Ela's place across the Bosphorus.
But I gave up on the idea.

I kept carrying books.
Sweat was pouring down from my legs,

pain dug into my arms and shoulders,
but I pushed on.

I had even started to take pleasure in the pain in my shoulders —
it made me feel alive, made me feel I existed.

By the final trip, it was nearly six o'clock.
I collapsed onto the floor.

The table was full,
and piles of books lay scattered across the living room.
I reeked of sweat, soaked through.

I wasted no time and jumped into the shower.
Afterwards, I lay down and rested for a while.
When I felt better, I got up and got dressed.
It was already seven — time to go out.

And I left.

If Ela had been with me then,
I would have said,
"Let this be our last day."

And when she asked,
"Where?"

I would have answered,
"There."

She would laugh and ask again,
"Where?"

And again I would answer,
"There."

And there would be endless.
It would never end.

Now I'm alone again, wandering the streets.
These Beyoğlu streets —
they're a woven net.

If only I could walk Sadri Alışık Street one last time, and
the street would end…
The road would end…
Humanity would end…

If only I could stand before the Ağa Mosque and say:
"Which part of you is a mosque, really?"
And if the mosque could answer:
"And which part of you is human?"

I wouldn't listen —
I'd just keep walking.
Toward Taksim this time.

Taksim comes too fast.
People flow from Taksim toward me,
people pour down Istiklal Avenue, scattering out to the world.

I'm hungry too — of course I am.
Hours of hauling weight.

Maybe I'll step into a street stall,
eat three wet hamburgers.
And if that's not enough,
maybe a döner wrap too.
Two ayrans to wash it down…

91

Then I turned back again, walking down Istiklal.
There's this intellectual bar Ahmet hangs out at —
maybe I should go there?
Where was that bar anyway?

Or maybe I should find Batu.
Yeah, he usually hung out at some bar down one of these side streets.
The bar was on the third floor.
You could barely even call it a bar.
It was just one big room.
In the corner, there was a bar counter, like a kitchen countertop just thrown together.
The bartender was one of us —
a bearded guy.

Yeah, I'm lucky — Batu was there, at the bar.
The tables were scattered all around, like some village coffeehouse.
He hugged me tight.
He was my close buddy from Ankara.

I had even gone to his wedding.
The girl was ugly, but she was rich.
Batu himself came from a wealthy family too,
but he wasn't some snobby bourgeois type —
he was a real stand-up guy.

- "So, what did you guys do after the wedding?"
- "We went to America, man."
- "What the hell were you doing in America?"
- "Just hanging out in New York…"
- "And money? How did you survive?"
- "Man, I found this killer job…"
- "What kind of job?"
- "I washed dead bodies, dressed them up, perfumed them, did their makeup, tucked them into coffins. Hahaha... You wouldn't believe the money!"
- "Bullshit. No way."
- "I swear, man. Made a ton, but we blew it all, me and the wife."
- "Where's the wife now?"
- "She's back in Ankara. I'm hanging around here for a few months."
- "Best thing you could do."
- "Man, remember the night we almost jumped off the roof of Rodhaus? Hahaha!"
- "If we had jumped, we wouldn't be here now."
- "Hahaha, totally! We were totally wasted. Why'd you come after me anyway?"
- "Man, I had this dream about you the night before. I guess blood called to blood.
  Then when I saw you heading up the stairs from the

bar, I thought, 'He's gonna fly, he's lost it,' so I followed you..."
- "Hahaha, you're a legend, man. Anyway, come on, let's get some tequila shots."
- "Alright. Ziya, two tequilas!"
- "You gotta cut it with lemon first, otherwise beer messes up your stomach. You know how this works."
- "Hahaha, of course I do. Man, how's work with you?"
- "Yeah, I quit the site. Long story. Couldn't take it anymore. Now I'm just hanging out, doing nothing. Gonna start looking for a new job soon."
- "So you're staying in Istanbul."
- "That's the plan."
- "What about that deal with Deniz, the house?"
- "Man, it didn't work out. I left. Got my own place in Çukurcuma."
- "Nice! That suits you. Write the address down here, maybe I'll swing by tomorrow."
- "Come by, man. It's a good spot."
- "Deniz was a tough one. I always knew you guys wouldn't last. Haha..."
- "Yeah, mainly a money thing. Otherwise, we were good."
- "Bullshit, man. Don't feed me that. You moved out!"
- "Whatever. Forget it. Let's get another round of tequila."
- "..."
- "..."

- "Cheers, bro."
- "Cheers. Down the hatch!"
- "Ehhh... downing it feels good."
- "Yeah, there's no other way."
- "Man, you still writing poetry? Bring some tomorrow."
- "I will. I got one on me right now — look, it's in my pocket, scribbled on some paper."

92

Vatman
This tram — where does it go?
Same road, back and forth.
Blow your whistle, let these idiots hear it.
Vatman
Whose ass does this tram ride?
Whose face does it slap?
Where does this road even lead?
Do those who leave ever come back?
Do those who come ever leave again?
How many hours is this tunnel back-and-forth?
Vatman
Don't look at me like that...
Just go, man — who can stop you?

- "Man, this is insane! Hahahah.

- What — you fell in love with the vatman or something?
- Hahah, what are you even talking about!
- When you said 'back and forth', I thought maybe you lost your mind.
- Hahah, you're the one who's high. Shall we keep going with the tequila?
- Keep it coming, of course!
- Just keep 'em coming as fast as you can."

Batu and I talked for another hour or so.
After the tequila, we each had one more beer.
Then I left.
The tequila had blown the dust out of my lungs, made me forget my tiredness.
I was heading toward the bar under Atlas Cinema.
Maybe Deniz would be there.
I wanted to see her.
If Ela had been with me, she would have said, "Let this be our last night."
That's why I needed to see Deniz — to make peace somehow.

We had spent so many nights at that bar together — laughter, wildness, those endless nights.
It made sense to find her there.

It was a long, narrow place.
When I entered, I walked through the whole bar, table by table.

Then I ducked into the restroom.
No Deniz.

Frustration welled up.
I sat down at the bar.
Ordered a small beer.
I wasn't even looking around.
My eyes were locked on the beer glass.

It looked like a whirlpool —
a golden whirlpool, crowned with foam.
A deep world inside that glass.
I wanted to dive in, sink to the bottom.
But I didn't.
Couldn't.

I wondered —
how could I be so full of life and still so utterly alone?
Was it youth that was like this?
Or life itself?
I didn't know.

If I cried, I could have filled the beer glass.
But I wasn't crying.

93

Maybe I would have cried on Ela's shoulder.
What kind of organization was I part of?
What kind of brotherhood?
Did brothers really leave each other this alone?
What were we even doing — I still didn't understand.

I understood the meaning, the goal,
but not the method.
We were supposed to protect our cell.
But when you weren't in action, protection was easy —
because there was no risk, no danger.
Was all this just preparation for some other time?
Someone should have explained more to me...

I was lost in these thoughts when suddenly someone
smacked my shoulder.
I turned around.
It was Deniz.

She always did that — hit you first, then laugh and say,
"What's up, man?"
And I would laugh too.
It happened exactly like that again.
Then she stepped back a bit, bounced on her toes like she
always did, lifted her right arm, and said:
"Where the hell have you been? You disappeared."

I was stunned for a second.
She wore cropped orange pants, almost fluorescent green t-shirt, and the same worn, purple canvas shoes she always wore.
In her left hand, she was carrying a beige cardigan.

"I'm around. I haven't disappeared," I managed to say
quietly.
She came and sat on the barstool next to me.

"Come on, buy a beer," she said.
"Two beers," I told the bartender — mine was almost empty too.
"Make it big ones! What's this tiny crap!" she shouted.
"Make it two big beers," I repeated.

Our beers arrived.
I told her I'd quit the job,
that Ela and I had rented a new place together.
She asked about Ahmet.
"I don't see him much anymore," I said.
Apparently, Ahmet wasn't calling her either.

Deniz had taken on two more roommates after I left,
to ease the rent burden.
Her master's at Marmara was going well;
she had started working part-time at an agency.
She was doing fine —
everything seemed good...

When her friends showed up, we stood up.
It was about that time in the night anyway when everyone started standing.
Her friends never really liked me much.
And I was getting drunk.
I could have gotten argumentative.

So I didn't stay long.
I kissed Deniz on the cheek and left.

94

I started walking along İstiklal again.
Now I wanted to find Bahadır. I headed to the little booth phone cabins next to Galatasaray High School.
I bought a token from the kiosk and called him.
He answered, cheerful and slightly drunk,
"We were just about to leave," he said.
"Where to?" I asked.
He named some club.
"Okay, pick me up in front of Galatasaray as you pass," I said.
He didn't sound too happy about it—tried to dodge me—but I was already annoyed and insistent.
"Pick me up, man," I said and hung up.
I stood waiting at the school gate, watching people pass by, waiting for someone, standing like a stone.

After a while I got bored.
I wandered into Çiçek Pasajı, bought a slim cigar from a kiosk, and lit it.
I strolled through the passage into the fish market, looped back to İstiklal, and resumed standing guard at the gate.
Half an hour passed—still no sign of them.
If I called again, they'd probably already have left.
But Bahadır wouldn't ditch me—he couldn't.
I kept waiting.
Fifteen minutes later, he appeared, with a girl on his arm.

The girl was big-boned—
Not fat, but wide-shouldered, tall, with long straight dark hair,

And the smell of perfume poured over her.
You could tell she came from money.
Bahadır was excelling in his flirtation career, mostly
targeting rich girls.
Some kind of modern gigolo institution...
And he was good at it.

It wasn't my style, but he was my childhood friend.
We'd started this whole nightlife thing together, built our
theories together, shared knowledge and war stories.
It had been useful.

We started walking toward Tünel.
Bahadır wrapped his right arm around the girl's waist and
slung his left arm around my shoulders.
He briefly introduced her.
He usually tried to keep his girls away from me—
I didn't mind; our tastes were different.
He knew how to dress up and sell himself;
I usually looked like a construction worker next to him.

Getting into the club without them would've been
impossible,
But with Bahadır it was easy:
He had connections, charisma, paid the door fee, and we
got in smoothly.

They were already tipsy, maybe more—
Maybe they'd smoked something too.
I was slower, heavier.
So I headed straight for the bar, separating from them.

I wanted to keep drinking—
Switch to whiskey.

They disappeared into the crowd, dancing to the music.
I had no intention of joining any group.
If anything, I wanted to crash into everyone and no one.
It was past 12:30.
The night was just starting there.

The door kept letting more people in.
Girls—
So many girls—
And each one stunning, each different, each magnetic.
I was trying to catalogue them all with my eyes—
But they all seemed so far away, like visitors from another planet.

A deep sense of inadequacy started to creep in.
I found a barstool in the farthest corner and sat down.
The disco ball spun overhead,
The world spun,
My head spun.

As the place packed tighter, I kept drinking whiskey,
Never leaving my spot.

Eventually it got so crowded that from where I sat, I couldn't even see the dance floor anymore.

The male-to-female ratio was still male-heavy,
But better than average.

Some rowdy guys bumped into me, laughing, trying to push me aside—
I was getting irritated.
I ordered another double whiskey—heavy on the ice—
And left the bar.

Wading into the crowd now,
Drink in hand, moving with the beat like everyone else.
Somewhere in the mess, Bahadır and the girl had gotten lost in another group.

The last whiskey really hit me.
Now a sick, sloppy grin spread across my face.
The shame turned to disdain.
I started seeing everyone through a dirty lens:
The women seemed like careless whores;
The men drooling scavengers,
Sniffing around like wild dogs.
Everyone saw themselves in some fake mirror.
There was no reality left.

They had all collapsed into something stupid, soft, ridiculous.

They deserved to be crushed,
Stomped on.
All of them.

When I finished my drink,
I left my glass wherever and staggered toward the restroom.

Even standing next to another guy at the urinal irritated me.
I wanted to sock him in the mouth.
I stared at him sideways, fiercely.
He averted his eyes.

Coming out, I realized my hands were empty.
Back into the crowd,
I noticed there was another bar under the mezzanine I
hadn't seen before.

It was packed.
I muscled my way through, handed the bartender cash, and
ordered a beer.
He passed me a bottle—already opened—gave my change.
I got the hell away from the crowd.

Time to dive back into the dance floor,
Into the pit.

Beer in hand, I waded into the mob.
Everyone swayed.
I swayed.
I grinned at everyone now.

I sidled up to random girls.
They ran away.
I cursed under my breath.
Kept dancing, kept swaying.

At some point, I found Bahadır again—
He and his girl had formed a circle with others,
And Bahadır was in the center, showing off.

It was pathetic, hilarious.
When he spotted me, he rushed over, grabbed me into a hug—
Genuine affection.

I danced with them for a bit,
Then broke off, went for another beer.
Another beer after that.
And the floor again.
And another beer.
And the floor again...

95

After that, there are no records.

When I started regaining consciousness, I found myself in Çukurcuma, outside Bahadır's place, the two of us wrestling.
We weren't hitting each other exactly, just shoving and scuffling.
Bahadır was shouting, *"F... off! F... off already!"*
I must have pushed him to the edge, must have vomited all my hatred onto him.
His rich, big-assed girlfriend was nowhere to be seen.

Suddenly my mind cleared.
"Fine," I said. *"I'm leaving. But I'm never going anywhere with you again."*
And I started walking toward my place.
Luckily, it was nearby.

96

When I woke up, I was home.
Though calling it "waking up" wasn't quite right—
It was more like surfacing from a deep coma.
The familiar pounding headache was back.

I dragged myself into the shower.
As I sobered up a little, the full force of the headache came crashing in—
It was unbearable, but somehow I always endured it.
I dried off, struggled into some clothes, and stepped outside.

The sunlight stabbed my eyes, making the pain worse.
I made it to a pharmacy, bought two boxes of aspirin and two boxes of Alka-Seltzer.
Then I stopped by the greengrocer: tomatoes, cucumbers, lemons.
Then the market: cheese, bread, yogurt, five bottles of water, plenty of soda water.
Finally, I dragged myself back home.

I squeezed an entire lemon into a beer glass,
Slowly poured soda over it.
It foamed up violently—
I set it aside to settle.

In a second beer glass, I filled it with water and dropped in two effervescent aspirin tablets.
I drank half the soda-lemon mix, then drained the aspirin cocktail.

Changed into sweatpants, lay down.
But the headache and hangover wouldn't let me sleep.

I got up again, finished the rest of the soda-lemon.
Wandered over to the piles of books in the living room.
Sat at the table, picked up books at random, leafed through five or ten of them.
Put them back on the shelves.
Sat again.
Looked.
Got up again and reshuffled the shelves.

My vision was sharpening, but my stomach was a wreck.
I went back to the kitchen.
Ate a little bread and cheese.
My mouth dried up immediately.

I made another soda-lemon mix.
Dropped an Alka-Seltzer into a water glass—watched it bubble.
Drank the Alka-Seltzer.
Took a swig of soda-lemon on top.

Back to the books.
Kept organizing in the same slow, semi-conscious pattern.

By noon, the doorbell rang.
I hoped it was Afet—
Whenever I was this hungover, my libido went wild.
All I wanted was to fuck and keep fucking until the pain drained out of me.

I opened the door.
It was Batu.
He looked just as destroyed and hungover as me.

Still, I was glad to see him.
"What's up, bro?" he said, walking in.
"Eh, rough hangover," I answered.

He stepped into the living room.
"What the hell happened here?" he asked, looking at the piles of books.
"Nothing much," I said.

"Got anything to eat?" he asked.

We moved to the kitchen.
I dumped cucumbers, tomatoes, cheese, and yogurt onto the counter.
Without a word, Batu rinsed the cucumbers, grabbed a knife, and started peeling them.

His hands were shaking as he peeled four cucumbers.
Then he quartered them lengthwise.
Pulled down a plate from the shelf and arranged the slices neatly.

"Got salt?" he asked.
I handed him the salt shaker.

He salted each cucumber slice carefully, one by one,
Then set the plate and the yogurt on the table.

Next, he grabbed the bread, sliced it up, placed it on the table.

"Come on, bro, let's eat," he said.

We sat across from each other at the kitchen table.

"Want me to bring the cheese and tomatoes too?" I asked.
"Nah, no need," he said. *"We're both wrecked. Gotta go easy on the liver, clean out the system. This is perfect."*

We each grabbed a cucumber slice, scooped up yogurt, and started eating.

Between bites, Batu started talking about alcohol, about addiction...

97

"Bro, you really went off the rails last night, didn't you?"
"Don't even ask. First tequila with you, then I moved over to Atlas, kept going with beer, then hit some club—can't even remember the name—and switched to whiskey, finished with more beer. Of course I blacked out."
"Hahaha, classic you, man. Classic me too..."
"And you?"
"I was at Kahve Bar the whole night. Tequila, beer, and whatever else people bought me."
"Dude, your hands are shaking bad..."
"Yeah, it's hereditary. Only in the mornings though. Let me eat a bit, I'll be fine."
"You want an Alka-Seltzer or an aspirin? Or maybe a soda

with lemon?"
"Alka sounds good."

I got up and made him a glass of Alka-Seltzer.
We couldn't eat much—our stomachs were still wrecked.
Afterwards, we moved to the living room, to the table.
Batu started browsing the books while I kept shelving them.

"Bro, why so many shelves?"
"There's a reason..."

Batu, now tired of drinking, had turned his energy to poetry.
He was reading poems—some of his own, some from the books stacked on the table.

He was especially hooked on Ece Ayhan.
"Bro, you know what? I'm going to visit Ece Ayhan next week."
"No way, that's awesome!"

Batu's favorite poet had always been Ece Ayhan.
There was an Ece Ayhan book lying on the table too.
He kept reading from it.

"Bro, the man's a giant. The real deal. You know, he always said, 'I'm not a poet, I'm an ethicist.'"
...

By the time Batu left, it was nearly five o'clock.
I had managed to flush out some of the alcohol with all the

water and soda.
Now, my body—and even more so, my soul—was craving real sleep.
As I drifted off, my mind was full of Ela—
but my body was still yearning for Afet.

I finally fell asleep around six.

98

I woke up at 3 a.m.
I had slept enough.
I got up and brewed some tea.
I continued working on the books.
Without rushing, reading a little here and there, but without sticking to any strict order, I placed the books the way I had seen them arranged in the central cell—without ever going back.
Wherever I put a book, it stayed.
By 8 a.m., it was done.
All the books were shelved, yet even half the shelves weren't full.
I was exhausted.
I lay back down.
This time, I fell into a deep sleep.

Waking up was a struggle.
I could hear sounds, little taps and noises, but I couldn't wake up enough to check.
My body wouldn't obey my mind's commands.

My body wanted to rise, but my mind wouldn't let go of the dreams.
I was glued to the bed, as if bound with some sticky glue of my own making.
There was no getting up—
Was it because getting up would mean the end of everything?
I wasn't going to fight it.
I laid my head against the soft chest of sleep and let myself drift.

I heard the door to the room open—
but I told myself it was part of the dream too and didn't even turn around to look.
Then the light switched on.
When I opened my eyes, I was met with the glaring white of the wall.
Now I realized it wasn't a dream at all, but I didn't panic.
Slowly, I turned from the wall to face the room.
There, standing in front of me, was a tall girl.

"*Who are you?*" I said, struggling to open my eyes.
"*Of course you wouldn't recognize me,*" she said. "*You forget so easily...*"

I managed to sit up a bit, leaning my back against the wall.
I stared more carefully.

"*Come on, look closer,*" she said, "*it's me, Afet—how could you not recognize me?*"

Now I could see her clearly—
yes, it was Afet, but she was completely transformed.
She wore fitted jeans—tight but not too tight—high heels on her feet,
a sleeveless top, and over that a short jacket.
Her hair was done up—washed, blown out, shining black.
She had a touch of makeup, red lipstick, and a scent that filled the whole room, overpowering even the sweaty smell I had left behind.

She was someone else now.
I got even more excited.
I sat up fully.

"Wow... what did you do to yourself? You look like a completely different person!"

Afet had shifted her weight onto one leg, her hands on her hips, lightly swinging her leg.

"Ugh, I got tired of being the gypsy girl," she said, *"It's Sunday today, figured I'd give myself a Sunday holiday— threw off those rags, dressed up, went to the hairdresser, and came straight to you."*

99

"You did well," was all I could say.
"I'll go take a shower then," I said.
Afet smiled. *"Okay, I'll look through the books while you're in there. You've arranged them nicely."*
I felt ashamed of myself, standing next to her I felt like

some street kid.
Normally, I would undress in the room before heading to the bathroom, but somehow, I felt shy around Afet now. After she left the room, I grabbed my towel and quietly went to the bathroom.
I shaved and took a shower.
Moving just as quietly, I slipped back into the room and put on a clean pair of jeans and a shirt.
Afet was in the living room, flipping through the books. When she saw me, she smiled.

Was this the same girl?
How could someone change this much?
I hardly dared to touch her.

"The books look beautiful," she said.
"They'll look even better once the shelves are full," I replied.
"Yes," she said, *"this will be a beautiful cell."*
"Yes..."

I started browsing the books alongside her, bending down next to her, reaching out for the same books she tried to pull out, brushing against her hand.
She would smile, flashing those bright, perfectly white teeth.
A little bit of lipstick had smudged onto one of her teeth.
"Wait," I said, gently pulling her to face me.
I wiped the smudge away with the tip of my pinky finger.
She had taken off her jacket.
Her tanned skin seemed different now, even compared to the first time we had made love.

I wanted her—but I didn't want to rush to touch her in this state.
We kept talking about the books.

Later, we sat at the table, just talking.
Time passed.
"Are you hungry?" Afet asked suddenly.
I was starving.
"Starving," I said.
She jumped up and ran to the kitchen. I followed.
"Let's make menemen," she said. *"You start the tea. I'll run and grab the missing stuff. Then I'll cook."*
"Alright," I said.

She threw on her jacket and went out.
I put the tea on to brew.
I was still stunned by her.
She returned carrying a huge grocery bag.
She did all the cooking.
We ate together.

Then she said, *"Come on, let's lie down."*
"Alright," I said.

We went to the floor mattress.
I lay down first, against the wall, then she slipped off her shoes and lay down beside me.
I couldn't wait any longer.
I leaned over and kissed her on the lips.
A damp kiss.
Her breathing immediately changed.
She looked into my eyes through a haze.

I kissed her again.
Then she kissed me back.

We kissed for a long, long time...
And then, slowly, piece by piece, we undressed each other, cleansing ourselves of every bit of dirt, until we were bare and clean.

When we paused after making love, lying side by side staring up at the ceiling, I said:
"You can't be Afet. You're someone else. What's your real name?"

She turned to me and smiled:
"I'm Şükran. My name is Şükran," she said.

Şükran stayed with me all day in the cell.
She left early Monday morning, around six.
"I still have to change my clothes," she said, laughing.

I kept sleeping after she left.
Waiting for the evening to come, waiting for time to pass.

I didn't leave the house all day,
I waited with the books.

Time was on my side.
That day, evening arrived very, very late.

100

Around six, Ela called.
"I'm leaving at six, I'll come straight to your place," she said.
Waiting had worked—time had been defeated.
"Okay," I said.
As always, she wasn't late.
Within half an hour, there was a knock at the door.
She entered with her sad, heavy face.
"Where should we sit?" she asked.
We moved to the kitchen, sat at the kitchen table.
I poured us both some tea.

I started talking—
I hadn't planned this conversation to go this way.
"Two days ago, when I found your letter in the drawer, I thought I would love you forever. I thought I already did, endlessly... But my perceptions and concepts have been shifting so fast lately. Today, I'm at a completely different point. This has nothing to do with love or not loving you. I'm tangled in something I can no longer even express. I am no longer myself. I still love you—but I can't pull you into this... I shouldn't."

Ela's misty eyes began to fill with tears.
Her lips trembled as she asked questions, trying to understand.
But trying to understand—what a futile effort that was.
I couldn't explain.
She couldn't understand.
There were no words left to say.

It was simply over.
It had ended.
That's all.

101

Designs for life...

They can cause someone to leave your life.
When the designs and expectations no longer match reality,
deep unhappiness inevitably follows.

Ela's departure left a landslide inside me.
In the days that followed, I couldn't leave the house.
I only went out to the market and the greengrocer.
I wasn't drinking—
The effects of my last binge had lasted for days.
For a week, I was plagued by burning headaches and an aching body...

On the other hand, I wasn't completely alone:
There was Afet.
There was Marina.
There was our cell.
There was our brotherhood...

Yet days passed—
and neither Marina nor Afet appeared.
Every night I would tell myself:
"Tomorrow, Afet will come for sure,"
or
"Tomorrow, Marina will slip a note under the door."

But each new day came and went,
and nothing happened.

I lost track of how many days or weeks had passed.
Now, I would go to the old house every day too,
hoping, just maybe, that a note from Marina would have
been left there.

Then, I would wander the streets—
aimless, endless walks through all the alleys of Beyoğlu,
especially our neighborhood, through the web of streets
that felt woven around me.

All I wanted was to see Afet again.
To find her.
It wasn't just Afet anymore—
it felt like all the Gypsies had vanished into thin air.

From then on, Tarlabaşı became my home.
If a day passed without me walking its streets, searching
every girl's face, every child's eyes for a glimpse of Afet,
I couldn't find peace.

I walked through street after street,
down to the farthest alleys,
learning every corner by heart—
but I could never find the cell house again.

*"Where are you?
Where?"*

I wanted to scream it—
but the words choked in my throat.

What was this longing?
For whom—or for what—was I aching?
I no longer knew.

102

...

Ela wasn't calling.
Neither was Ahmet.
Nor Deniz.

In the evenings, I would go out, bar-hopping —
entering places just to look, then leaving again.
I would stand at the doors of taverns,
then move on.

No one was there.
Not Bahadır,
not Batu —
I never ran into anyone.
It was as if the whole world was playing hide and seek with me...
Everyone couldn't have simply disappeared, evaporated.

I had grown afraid of even glancing at time, at history.
Days and hours passed in a scale-less, shapeless flow for me...

The books sat on the shelves, exactly as I had arranged them,
but I couldn't bring myself to touch them.

It was becoming impossible to endure these days,
this time,
this waiting,
this longing — without alcohol.
I couldn't cope.

Every morning,
I would go out and buy the cheapest wine, the cheapest beer,
and the cheapest cigarettes.
I started drinking in the morning.

The only food I could manage to eat was boiled eggs and boiled potatoes.
Nothing else would go down my throat.

Most days, I couldn't even get out of the floor mattress.
My hair and beard had become a tangled mess.
Taking a shower felt like the hardest thing in the world.

If I could manage to get outside,
I would walk for hours.
If not —
the nights and mornings blurred into each other,
countless and uncounted...

There was still one reality threatening all of humanity:
poverty.
And it was dragging me, too, back toward "normal" life.

My money was running out.

The rent was due —
I had paid it once,
but now the second month's rent was looming.

Marina had said, *"Don't worry about money."*
But Marina was gone.

Ela had said, *"We'll share it, I'll help."*
But Ela was gone too.

Ahmet had said, *"The company will support you."*
But I no longer had a job —
nor a company.

103

One morning, very early,
I woke up and went to my barber,
the one on the side street near Nevizade.

He was very old —
only he would open that early,
at six in the morning.
I got there around 6:30.

When he saw me, he smiled —
but he couldn't help asking about my state.
He was surprised.

"I've been sick," I said.
His hands were trembling as he shaved me.

I went back home, took a shower, changed my clothes,
then went out and bought every newspaper with job
listings.

I collected fax numbers
and sent out my resume from a small stationery shop I
knew in Cihangir.

This became my new daily routine.
A few days later, the first phone call came,
and I started going to interviews.

My days were now spent on buses,
minibuses, ferries —
constantly searching for addresses in the vast ocean of
Istanbul.

After five interviews,
I stopped applying altogether.

I went back to waiting at home, drinking,
waiting for some news —
and drinking more while I waited.

I was slowly returning to my old state.
No one was calling.
I couldn't find a job.

After a while,
I applied to every listing again.
This time, only one person called —
but I didn't go.
I couldn't go.

It just wasn't happening.

The company had deposited my final paycheck,
along with the rent support they had promised for the last few months.

I had managed to pay the rent —
a little late,
but paid.

Now, the next rent was three weeks away,
and I knew whatever money I had left wouldn't be enough.

If I couldn't find a job,
paying the rent would be impossible.

So I kept drinking.
I couldn't bear to stay in the apartment anymore.

Longing and waiting had taken over my entire mind.

I would wake only in the afternoons,
wander the streets.

My range was expanding:
all of Çukurcuma, Cihangir, Tarlabaşı,
from Tünel all the way down to Karaköy —
I was everywhere.

But they weren't.

The people I loved had vanished.

I started finding the darkest, cheapest bars
and sitting there.
Drinking tea in tea houses.
Smoking endless cigarettes.

No matter how much I called out to them with my entire
being —
they didn't come.

People wouldn't even talk to me anymore.
Maybe they were afraid I would infect them with whatever
disease I carried.
Maybe I was afraid too.

104

One night,
I drank until very late at Kahve Bar,
hoping Batu might show up.

Batu would have been the only one who could make me
feel a little better.

But the bartender said,
"Don't bother waiting, man. Batu left Istanbul."

Still, I had nowhere else to go —
so I kept drinking.

Around four in the morning,
I finally stumbled out.

My money was almost gone.
I withdrew some cash from an ATM
and headed toward home,
cutting through Sadri Alışık Street.

As I passed by Bonbon,
a thought struck me —
Marina.

That first night she came to me,
and everything that followed.

I couldn't resist.
I went in.

They didn't greet me warmly this time.
İsmail Ağa was gone.
Most of the staff had changed.

My eyes started scanning the tables —
looking for a place to sit.

In one of the back booths,
there was a woman who looked eerily like Marina.
She was sitting across from a man,
but I couldn't see his face.

I moved to the other side of the club,
found a spot where I could watch them without being noticed.

I ordered a beer,
paid for it immediately,
and started watching.

It *was* Marina.

The man's face was still hidden,
but after a while, he shifted slightly —
turning to his left.

That's when I saw him clearly.

It was Ahmet.

105

When I saw Ahmet and Marina together,
I bolted out of there.

I started walking fast toward home,
but after a while,
I realized I could hear the footsteps of three people behind me.

I didn't care.
My mind was too full —
spinning with what I had just seen.

I was so distracted that I missed my turn home
and kept walking down toward Bahadır's place,
deeper into Çukurcuma.

It was five in the morning.
The footsteps behind me grew louder, closer,
but I still didn't pay them any attention.

I was lost in my own head.

When the footsteps were almost at my side,
I instinctively turned around.

One of them said,
"Hey, brother, hold up a second!"

"What's up?" I said.

Another pulled out a switchblade.

I stepped back reflexively.
"Relax, what do you want?" I said.

The other two also pulled out knives.

"Hand over everything you've got," one of them said.

I calmly took out my wallet.
I gave them all the cash inside.

"Give us the wallet too," another one demanded.

I handed it over.

They took my bank cards as well,
leaving me with just my ID,
and tossed the empty wallet back to me
before running off down into the lower streets of Çukurcuma.

I stood there, not knowing what to do.

Eventually,
I turned around and walked quickly back up toward Sadri Alışık Street,
heading straight for the police station.

I told them what had happened.

"Do you want to file an official complaint?" they asked.

"Of course," I said.

They took me into a small room.
There was only a large table inside.
They placed several thick photo albums in front of me.

*"Go through these. If you recognize anyone,
write the number down here."*

I started flipping through the albums.
Hundreds of faces stared back at me
with blank, empty eyes.

I kept looking…
but after a while, my stomach began to turn.
I couldn't stand those eyes looking back at me anymore.

I left the room
and went to where the officers were sitting.

"I'm withdrawing my complaint," I said.

"Alright," one of them said,
tearing up my paperwork without any fuss.

I left and walked back home.

By the time I got there,
the sky had already started to lighten.

I waited for the banks to open.
Around eight o'clock,
I left again and went to the bank.

I told them I had lost my card,
and asked them to check my account.

All the money was gone.
Zero balance.

I went back home.

106

I slept a little.
Took a shower.
Packed my bag and gathered my things.

There was a small amount of emergency cash I had left in
the apartment.
In the afternoon, I called Ela.

"You have to come over tonight," I said.
"Why?" she asked.
"Just come. It's important."
"Okay," she said.

Until Ela arrived, I cleaned and tidied up the place.
Everything I owned fit into one suitcase.
I was going to leave my books behind.

She came around eight o'clock —
she had stayed late at work.

"I'm leaving," I told her,
"Going back to Ankara.
I can't stay here anymore."

She was sad, but silent.
I handed her the key.
I told her I had already paid the last month's rent.
The rental contract was in both our names anyway — there wouldn't be any issues.

"Don't worry. I'll take care of it," she said.

I gathered my courage and asked,
"One more thing — do you have any cash on you?
I've got very little left.
I don't know if I can even buy a bus ticket."

"I don't have any with me, but I'll withdraw some," she said.
"Okay, let's head out together then, and you can grab it on the way," I said.

I loaded my suitcase,
locked the door,
gave her the key.

We walked up to İstiklal Avenue.
Ela stopped at a bank, withdrew some money, and handed it to me.
"I'll send it back once I find a job," I said.
"It's fine. Don't worry about it," she replied.

I dropped her off at the Bostancı minibus stop by AKM.
We hugged.
She left.

There was a bus company office in Gümüşsuyu
with hourly departures to Ankara.

I bought a ticket and waited for the shuttle.
The shuttle came and took us to the main bus station.

When I leaned my head against the window,
I finally felt calm — cooled by the glass.
The best thing was sleep.

And I drifted away…

—

In Ankara,
my old student apartment was still there —
and my family had moved into it while I was away,
but since it was summer, they had gone back to our hometown.

I was alone.

I had returned to "normal."
I was looking for work.
I wasn't drinking.

I kept thinking about what had happened,
about everything that had passed through my hands,
and I tried to write some of it down.

Having my old room back —
the one filled with the objects I had saved since childhood —
and my old books around me,
gave me comfort.

I was calmer.
More domestic.
I read,
I wrote.

But that didn't mean I wasn't hurting.

I had lost so many people,
and so quickly.
Everyone I had loved in that short time was gone.

And I had lost the book brotherhood too —
that hopeful, almost mythical organization I had started to believe in.
They had disappeared too.

But youth was still giving me energy.
I wanted to find a job as soon as possible.
Maybe even find someone to love.

I loved beginnings.

107

In that calm, I had let my mind and brain rest for two weeks.
I was feeling better.
Then, one day, the phone rang.

It was Ela.

First, she asked how I was doing.
Then she said,
"I want to come and see you."

"Okay," I said.

That same night, she got on a bus.
The next morning, I met her on the Eskişehir road.
She threw her arms around my neck.

We went home.

As soon as we entered the apartment, we made love.
We spent the whole day in bed.
We had missed each other so much.

We talked about everything —
but not about us.
It was as if we were lovers again.

Ela stayed for two nights.
She was supposed to leave on the third day.

She told me she had quit the company too.

Two hours before her departure, we finally began talking about serious things —
analyzing, judging what had happened.

I thought it was unnecessary.
"Tell me exactly what you want," I said.

"This is what I want," she said.
"Let's walk out that door together, buy a ticket to a seaside town,
cut all ties with everyone and everything,
and start over from scratch.
Not in Istanbul, not in Ankara.
Somewhere no one knows us.
I want a brand-new life with you..."

I thought about it for a moment.

And I realized — I didn't want it.
As much as the idea of running away and starting fresh tempted me,
I couldn't do it.

Without even planning to, these words fell from my mouth:

"Ela, I can't do it.
I'm sorry, truly sorry that I can't."

She got angry.
She threw her things into her bag quickly, slung it over her shoulder.

*"You don't even have to walk me out.
I'll go.
You're a coward."*

And she left.

—

Two weeks after Ela left,
the friend who had first helped me get a job at the company called.

He was giving me updates about the company —
about the embassy project.

It wasn't going well.
It sounded like they were about to get kicked off the job.

I felt sad.

And then —
out of nowhere —
he dropped another piece of news I hadn't expected at all.

He didn't know about my relationship with Ela —
no one in the Ankara office did —
so he spoke freely:

*"You know that architect girl from the Istanbul site?
Your assistant?
She and Ahmet are getting married, did you hear?"*

108

I hadn't heard.
"No, I hadn't," I said, completely in shock.
"I have to go," I said, and hung up.

I didn't know what to think.
I was angry.
I felt tricked, betrayed —
but it was their choice.
There was nothing I could do.

That day, for the first time in a long time,
I drank.
And the more I drank,
the angrier and more furious I became.

That evening, I couldn't hold it in anymore.
I called Ahmet.
I said whatever came to my mouth —
cursed at him.

He tried to explain.
I cursed again and hung up.

And that's how I began erasing them from my mind...

—

The next day,
a company I had applied to through a middleman called.

I went for the interview.
They were positive.

The company was based in Ankara,
but the job was in Gaziantep.

I accepted.

I would spend two weeks in training in Ankara,
then leave for Antep.

I was starting next Monday.

But before I started work,
there was something else I had to do.
...

I immediately got on a bus to Istanbul.

I was heading straight to the new house.

I had hidden one copy of the spare key inside my suitcase.
If they hadn't changed the lock, I could still get in.

It was already dark when I arrived in Istanbul.

I went straight to the building.

The house was dark —
no lights on.

I climbed the stairs.
Inserted the key into the lock.
Turned it.

The door opened.

I slipped in quietly.
I had a small flashlight in my pocket.
I switched it on.

The shelves were full —
arranged in the same pattern as the cell house.

The apartment was spotless.

The mattress was still there in the room,
with the blanket carefully folded over it.

In the living room,
more chairs had been added around the table.
Newer ones, too.

The living room shelves were packed tight with books.

I had seen what I came to see.

Without taking any more risks,
I turned toward the door to leave.

There, right in front of the door,
was a white card —
similar to the ones that had been left for me before.

I picked it up.

My name was written on it.

I opened it and read:

"YOU ARE A NOMAD."
— MARINA

Made in the USA
Las Vegas, NV
13 May 2025